Cowboys Don't Cry

THE SHOOTING STAR TRILOGY
BOOK ONE

SAMANTHA MICHAELS

I have so many people to thank!
To my PA Ayana Guerra and the team at Carxander Publishing for
being amazing! I'd be lost without you.
To my street team, thank you for helping share and promote my books!
To my author besties, LaLa Montgomery and JJ Grice, I love and adore
both of you talented ladies. Read their books!!
I need to say a huge THANK YOU to my husband Matt and our dog
Holly. Now more than ever, you've shown me how much you love and
support me, and I couldn't love you more.
And, of course, the readers! Thank you so much for taking a chance on my
books and helping make a lifelong dream come true.

Prologue

JUDD

"Cowboys don't cry, son." My father's bitter words the day of Mom's funeral still sting my ears to this day. Sitting here alone, staring out my big bay window, I think about the events that led me to the small, rural town of New Holland, Pennsylvania. How could everyone, including the woman I was supposed to marry, turn on me, but forgive my father? At least he's where he belongs. Prison. How the fuck could he take my mother away from me?

For the first twenty years I've lived in Pennsylvania, I had no friends. Then, the couple who lived next door moved to Florida and the following winter, someone new moved in. I still remember that day. I took one look at him, with his long hair and knew he was going to be trouble. But when I saw him struggling to move his furniture in, I walked next door to give him a hand.

"Looks like you could use some help," I said.

"Thanks, man," my new neighbor said.

"Got a name?"

"Damien St. James."

"Pleasure. I'm Judd Walker."

We discovered we had a lot in common and became fast friends. Sadly, the biggest thing we had in common was being single. That is

1

until a fateful spring day. His crazy dog, Dave, knocked a woman down at the dog park. We were in Damien's back yard having a beer, shooting the shit when he told me what happened.

"You won't believe what Dave did," Damien said.

"Uh oh, what?" I asked.

"You know that sexy woman I told you about?"

"Yeah."

"Dave knocked her on her cute little ass today."

"Was she hurt?"

"Only her pride. I found out her name's Lexi."

"That's awesome. Hope it works out."

"Thanks, man."

It did work out and Lexi eventually moved in with Damien. I'm happy for him, but I miss my friend. He still invites me over, but I feel like a third wheel. Not to mention the pangs of jealousy when I see the two of them together and so clearly in love.

I'm just finishing up a long day's work on my farm and getting ready to head in for a shower. Owning a farm keeps me busy, but I do love my house. I have a large single floor home. The outside is covered in a beautiful stone façade and the inside has more than enough room for a lonely bachelor. As I'm walking toward my back door, I hear barking and look toward Damien's house. I see the most stunning woman I've ever laid eyes on. Her long blonde hair glimmers in the sun. Curiosity gets the best of me and I walk to the fence that joins our properties. The mystery woman's jaw drops when she sees me.

Lexi looks over and calls out, "Would you like to join us, Judd?"

I nod and climb over the fence. "Howdy, ma'am," I say to the pretty blonde.

She giggles but says nothing.

"Judd, this is my best friend, Melissa. Melissa, this is Judd Walker."

"A pleasure," I say as I take the pretty blonde I now know as Melissa's hand and kiss it.

She giggles again, but at least manages a hello this time.

"Can I get you something to drink?" Lexi asks me.

"Beer, please,"

"Coming right up. Mel, do you wanna help me?"

Melissa jumps up and follows Lexi inside. The ladies are laughing when they return, and I can't help but wonder what about. I imagine all the dirty things I'd like to do with Melissa. I wish I was good enough for someone like her. Damien told me she's the Chief Financial Officer at O'Laughlin Consulting, one of Pennsylvania's top accounting, finance and technology firms.

As I spend more time around Mel, my interest in her increases, but my willpower is strong. I feel she's into me, but she says nothing. Summer brings more of the same, including acting as Mel's date at their high school reunion. I get a glimpse of Mel's feisty side when Lexi's ex-boyfriend Bryan shows up with his girlfriend Amy, a former classmate of Mel and Lexi.

"Well, well, it's the reject table," Amy says.

"Fuck you, bitch," Mel says.

"Still classy, I see."

"What do you want?"

"To show the pig that Bryan has a real woman now."

"Too bad you don't have a real man. Hope you have a magnifying glass when you're in bed."

"Fuck off, bitch," Bryan snarls.

"Whatever, tiny," Melissa said.

Seeing her like that turns me on. I love a strong woman. Especially one as sexy as her.

One warm summer afternoon, I see Mel and Lexi in Damien's back-yard and something comes over me. I remember Damien telling me how much those two like reading dirty romance novels.

After saddling up my white stallion, Bruno, I remove my shirt and ride towards the fence. I see both ladies stare at me, mouths hanging open. Lexi stops after a minute, but Mel sits frozen in place. All I want at that moment is to have her riding behind me. If only.

As summer continues, Lexi and Damien have to travel to California for his high school music teacher and former mentor Jack's funeral, so I watch their dogs. I still remember the day Damien told me about Jack.

"So, tell me what your family was like," I say to Damien.

"My mom left when I was young, and my dad said it was because of me. His fists never let me forget. By the time I got to high school, I was a hellion and a bully. But Jack saw something in me. He was a former musician, and my attitude was something he'd seen a million times. He used my love of rock music to help me focus on something constructive. He was more of a father to me than my old man could have hoped to be."

"You're lucky to have had him." If only you knew what my father did.

With Damien and Lexi away, I haven't been able to see Mel and I miss her. That's when I remember Lexi telling me I could call Mel if I needed help with the dogs.

"Hello," Mel says.

"You busy? I'm dog-sitting and could use some help," I say.

"Is everything okay?"

"Yes, I could just use an extra set of hands." Preferably on my naked body.

"Okay, I'll stop on my way home from work."

Of course, I chicken out and don't ask her for a date. I like her too much to subject her to me. I'll just have to settle for the friendship forming between us. We continue to have encounters similar to this. Helping Damien plan his engagement with Lexi gave me yet another chance to spend time with her.

One afternoon, I'm sitting on my front porch when Mel pulls into the driveway. As soon as I see her face, I jump up out of my chair. She wipes her nose with a tissue as tears slide down her cheeks.

"What's wrong, sweetheart?" I ask.

She opens her mouth, but no words come out. I guide her to my porch swing, and we sit. Her body shakes as she sobs, her head buried in our hands. When she's able to compose herself, she says, "There's been an accident."

"What? Who?"

"Me and Lexi's former classmate Doug and his wife. They were crossing Main, and they were hit."

"Oh my god, that's awful. How are they?" I have a feeling I already know the answer. Mel buries her head into my shoulder, soaking my shirt. Pulling her into my arms, I whisper, "I'm so sorry. What can I do?"

After another long silence, Mel whispers, "How am I going to tell Lexi?"

I think back to how my father told me about Mom and pull Mel tighter against me. I pull my handkerchief out of my pocket and dry her cheeks. Even with the dark circles under her eyes and her red nose, she's still the most beautiful woman I've ever seen. "Do you want to come inside? I could make us some dinner."

"Thanks, but I just wanna go home."

I watch Mel, shoulders hunched, head hanging down, walk to her car. A couple of days later, I see Mel pull into Damien and Lexi's driveway after they get home from their trip. The thought of attending a funeral makes my blood run cold, but I need to be there for Mel. After the funeral, I drive the fifteen minutes to Mel's house, though I'm not really sure why. I just know it's where I need to be. I sit in her driveway just staring at her beautiful brick house. I finally will myself out of my truck. I walk up Mel's side and knock on her oak-colored front door.

"What are you doing here?" she says when she answers the door.

"Just wanted to check on you."

"That's so kind of you. You're a great friend."

"I feel the same about you. Until I met Damien, it had been a while since I had friends."

"What about before that?"

"When I lived in Texas, I had a lot of friends. The ranch community is tight-knit. But, cross them, and you're done."

"And you crossed them?"

"In their eyes."

"What happened?"

"Let's just say sometimes the past is best left there."

"I see."

After several minutes of awkward silence, I turn toward Mel's front door. "If you need anything, feel free to call," I say. Before she can respond, I race out the door and speed home. When I get back home, I check my voicemail.

"Mr. Walker, this is Warden Jackson Donnelly. I'm calling about your father, Martin Walker. Please return my call as soon as you can. You already have the number."

I pull the number up on my contact list and dial.

"George Beto Unit, Donnelly speaking."

"This is Judd Walker returning your call."

"Mr. Walker, the prison regrets to inform you that your father, Martin Walker, has passed."

"Can you tell me what happened?"

"He had a heart attack."

"Is there anything I need to do?"

"Yes, Mr. Walker. We'll need you to come to the prison. We have some documents we'll need signed."

"And there's no other way?"

"I'm afraid it needs to be in person."

"I'll be there as soon as I can get a flight."

After I disconnect, I find a flight the following afternoon. After packing, I see Damien and Lexi outside and walk over to the fence.

"Hey, man, come join us?" Damien asks.

"I can't. I just wanted to tell you I'm going away for a while. Could I ask a favor?"

"Of course."

"Could you take care of my animals while I'm gone?"

"Where are you going?" Damien asks.

"Texas."

"Why are you going there?" Lexi inquires.

"I have to take care of something?"

"What?" Lexi presses.

"Look, I just need to know if you can take care of my animals. I'm leaving in an hour. Here's all the instructions, including where to buy more food. I have an account, so you won't have to put out any money. I'm not sure how long I'll be gone."

"Umm, okay," Lexi says, her brow furrowed.

"Thanks," I say, walking away before they can ask me anything else.

When I land in Austin, I rent a car and drive right to the prison. After signing all the required paperwork, I check into a hotel. I have a meeting the next day with a lawyer to see what else I have to do. What I thought would be a quick visit turned into almost a month. I was never more relieved than when the plane touched down at Philadelphia International Airport. Austin was hell. Time clearly doesn't heal all wounds. All I want now is to be back on my farm, lost in my work.

CHAPTER 1

Judd

Waking up, I'm greeted by another beautiful fall morning in Pennsylvania. I prefer the East Coast weather to Texas since I've lived here. Looking next door, I see Damien and Lexi sitting outside enjoying coffee while their dogs, Dave and Maggie, play in the yard. If not for Dave and his antics, Damien and Lexi may never have met! I hear a car and when I see Lexi's best friend Mel. As always, she looks like a beautiful goddess. Her blonde hair is pulled into a ponytail and sways behind her as she walks. And damn, a woman in glasses turns me on big-time. She's dressed in a blue knee-length skirt, white blouse and fitted suit jacket. The outfit has her curves on full display and my mouth waters. Unable to resist, I walk to the fence that joins our properties and climb over.

"Howdy, blondie," I say.

"Don't howdy me," Mel snaps.

"I beg your pardon."

"You leave for a month without so much as a damn word. I thought we were friends."

"We are."

"Yeah, well, friends don't treat each other like that."

I nod, knowing damn well she's right. I just couldn't bring myself to face her. If anyone could have convinced me to spill my guts, it would've been her and I just didn't want to talk about it. "I'm sorry," I whisper.

"Whatever," Mel says and turns to Lexi.

"Um, can I get either of you coffee or something else to drink?" Lexi asks.

"Coffee, please." Mel says.

"Same for me." I say.

"Damien, would you mind helping me?" Lexi asks.

Mel walks to where the dogs are playing and bends down to pick up a tennis ball. Dave comes running full speed ahead and before anyone can react, she's on her cute little ass. She leans forward, grabbing her ankle and wincing. Never one to leave a damsel in distress, I walk down and pick her up and carry her to the table. The look on her face reminds me of the one I used to see on her.

Damien carries the tray outside and lays it on the table. "I'm so sorry. Are you okay, Mel?" Damien asks.

"No worries. I just twisted my ankle when I went down," Mel says.

"Dave can be overzealous," Lexi says. "I should know."

"He can, but he's such a handsome fella that all is forgiven. Thanks for helping me." Mel says coldly. Even her being pissed at me stirs something in my jeans. I feel my cheeks heat from how turned on I am. I haven't been with a woman since I left my previous home. Determined to never get hurt like I did back home in Texas, I've been able to resist the opposite sex, but this woman is making it difficult.

As we're sitting there enjoying our coffee, Lexi says, "What do you all think about a Halloween costume party at the club?" Lexi asks.

"I love costume parties!" Mel says.

"I was thinking maybe having a theme, like famous movie and TV couples or something." Lexi adds.

"Oh, I love that," Mel says. "I'm just bummed I won't be able to go."

"Why not?" I ask.

"I can't go alone." Mel says, a sad look in her eyes.

Before my brain stops me, my mouth says, "Well, ma'am, I'd be honored if you'd allow me to escort you. As friends, of course, but we could still pick out a couple to dress as."

"Are you sure? I'd hate to put you out." Mel responds.

"It sounds like fun, so I'd love for you to accompany me," I say. What the hell am I doing?

"Well, then, I accept." Mel says.

My heart skips a beat and I smile. Quickly, I recover and get my emotions in check. How am I going to handle a date with this stunning creature, even if it's just as friends? But, it's only one night and there will be a lot of other people around, so I'll manage. Lexi's voice snaps me out of my daydream.

"Okay, out with it," Lexi says to Damien.

"Can we please be Danny and Sandy from Grease?" Damien asks.

"Really?" Lexi asks. "You want me to be a goody-goody?"

"No silly. I want Sandy from that part at the end. I need to see you in the tight black pants and shirt. And please god, the red heels!" Damien says.

"That makes more sense," Lexi says. "I thought you wanted me to be pure Sandy."

"No way in hell you could pull that off," Damien laughs.

"What do you mean by that? I'm as innocent as they come!" Lexi says.

Mel laughs so hard that she snorts. And not a quiet snort. She lets out the loudest snort I've ever heard.

"Oh my god, I'm so sorry." Mel says, her cheeks beet red.

"I thought it was cute." I say. Did I really just say that? What the hell is this woman doing to me? I'm behaving like a damn teenager. And a horny one at that.

Damien's jaw drops and Lexi just sits there in silence, while Mel giggles again. The dogs bark, so Damien goes down to throw the ball for them and I join them. Lexi and Mel put their heads together, talking and laughing. I can only imagine who the subject of their talk is, after my idiotic display. They emit a laugh so loud, Damien and I stop and stare.

"Do we want to know what that's about?" I ask Lexi.

"Nope!" Lexi says.

The dogs have worn themselves out and no longer run after the ball. They curl up in a sunny spot in the yard's corner, so Damien and

I head back to the table. Just as we arrive, Mel looks down at her watch.

"I need to head out. I had the morning off, but I have a meeting this afternoon, so I need to go prepare." Mel says.

She tries to stand and winces in pain. "Shit, I twisted it a little worse than I thought."

"Allow me to help you to your car." I say.

Before Mel can answer, I carry her to her car, with Lexi and Damien following me. Lexi opens the door so I can set her down inside.

"Are you going to be okay when you get to work?" Lexi asks.

"All good. Thank you, Judd, for the help." Mel says, as she lowers her eyes and smiles.

I tip my hat and say, "My pleasure, ma'am."

After Mel pulls out of the driveway, I head back to my ranch. Trying to get Mel out of my head, I get back to work harvesting the crops that are ready, then cleaning the horse stalls. But, of course, no matter what I do, I can't stop thinking about Mel. She's unlike anyone I've ever known, and I want to know more. My mind quickly heads south. All I can think about is what it would feel like to kiss that woman. Lexi's never given many details, but I know Mel's been hurt. My brain can't fathom hurting someone like her. She deserves to be worshiped and I intend to do just that.

I finish up my work for the day and get undressed. Walking to the bathroom to shower, my mind is consumed with Mel. Always dressed so professionally, and damn I'm a sucker for a woman in glasses. Carrying her today, smelling her lilac scented shampoo, feeling her arms around my neck has me on sensory overload and my dick responds with a vengeance. Like I've been doing for far too many years, I take care of my own needs, then finish my shower. I'd give anything to feel Mel's naked skin against mine.

Feeling restless, I walk out back. As I'm gazing up at the night sky, I see a shooting star. I remember reading that seeing a shooting star is a sign of hope and new beginnings. Tears fill my eyes.

"Mom, I know that was you. I need your advice more than ever." Her voice fills my head, as I remember something she said to me often. Don't wait for good things to happen to you. Make them happen, my son. Now, I need to figure out how. The next morning, I walk over to the fence when I see Damien and Lexi outside. A little while later, Lexi heads out to pick up Mel for a shopping trip, so I chat with Damien.

"How's Mel's ankle?" I ask.

"Better. Lexi called her last night, and she could walk with no pain," Damien says.

"I'm glad."

"I've been wanting to ask you something..." Damien says.

"Shoot."

"Would you consider being the best man at Lexi's and my wedding?"

"I'd be honored."

"Great. Thanks, man. You'll be walking with Mel. Speaking of Mel, level with me, dude."

"What do you mean?"

"You got a thing for her, don't ya?"

"I can't."

"Why not?"

"I need to get back to work."

"Come on, man. I see the way you look at her."

"Let it go."

"You two belong together."

"Seriously, Damien, just fucking drop it. I gotta go." I storm off without another word. When lunch time rolls around and all I've accomplished is thinking about Mel, I hatch a plan to see her and head over to the fence.

"Lexi back yet?" I ask Damien.

"Nope, she texted and said they were going to have lunch. I was going to surprise them."

"Mind if I tag along?"

"Not at all. I bet Mel would love to see ya."

I wanna see her too.

When we get to the mall, Damien parks at the mall's entrance. As we're walking through the mall, we see Mel and Lexi turn and look at another girl. We're close enough to hear the conversation and my blood boils.

13

"Oh, look, someone let the pigs out of their pen," the girl says to Mel and Lexi.

"Seriously, that's all you got?" Lexi asks.

"Plenty more where that came from if you can take it," the girl says.

"If it makes you feel better about your pathetic existence, keep insulting me." Lexi says.

"Nothing to add, loser?" the girl says to Mel.

The girl's eyes go wide and her mouth drops open when we walk up to them. "Shit, they're hot. You know, the type of men neither of you would ever get with."

"Actually, you couldn't be more wrong." Damien says. "I don't believe we've had the pleasure. Damien St. James, future husband of this beauty."

Laying a hand on Mel's arm, I say, "Judd Walker, ma'am."

The girl's face turns bright red as a scowl appears on her face. Without a word, she turns on her heel and stomps away. I look at Mel just as a couple of tears spill over. She looks down at her feet, then walks over to a bench and sits down.

"What are you guys doing here?" Lexi asks.

"We decided we wanted to treat two pretty ladies to lunch." Damien says and puts his arm out, which Lexi accepts. I do the same with Mel, and the four of us walk down to the food court. Mel and Lexi sit down at a table while Damien and I go order. After we finish eating, Damien and I walk to his car, while the ladies head to where they parked. If anyone noticed Mel slip me a note, they said nothing.

After Damien drops me off, I finish up the work I have left and grab a shower. Sitting at my kitchen table, I stare at the piece of paper Mel slipped to me. Call me later. Even her handwriting is beautiful. After half an hour of arguing with myself, I grab my cell and dial her number.

"Hello," Mel says.

"Hi," I barely choke out. "Hope this is okay."

"I wouldn't have given you my number otherwise," she says.

Taking a deep breath, I ask, "Who was that girl at the mall today?"

"My younger sister, Trish."

"And that's how she talks to you?"

"Yeah."

"I'm sorry if I'm prying, but, well, why?"

"She blames me for everything bad that's happened in her life."

"That's total bullshit."

Mel sighs and before quickly changing the subject. "Tell me something about your life before you moved here."

"There's not much to tell."

"Oh, so we're back to that?"

"Back to what?"

"Keeping me in the dark. I'm beginning to wonder if we really are friends."

"That's not fair."

"Yeah, well neither is refusing to open up."

"Mel."

"Look, just forget it. I need to be up early for work." She disconnects before I can respond.

"Fuck, I'm an asshole," I shout to nobody.

* * *

Sitting on my porch, waiting for Damien to pick me up for our tux fitting, my mind won't stop thinking about Mel and that cute little giggle. I would give anything to hear that in bed. Fuck, this woman has a hold on me. And I have to break free. I just can't be the man she deserves, but damn, I want her. Damien pulls up to the house, and I get in his car.

"Hey man, thanks for doing this," Damien says.

"I'm honored you asked," I say. "Hey, can I ask you somethin'?"

"Shoot."

"Why isn't Mel with anyone?"

"I honestly don't know, man. Interested in her?"

"Just curious."

The rest of the groomsmen, Dean, Mikael, Andy, and Johnny, are pulling up as Damien parks. After we finish getting our measurements done, we head back out as Damien's treating us all to lunch. A few minutes later, a limo pulls up, followed by Mikael's wife Hannah. I look and see Johnny's wife Eden and Lexi with her. The ladies walk over and join us.

"Surprise! Welcome to your overnight bachelor party!" Dean says. "We arranged it with Lexi."

"Thanks, guys. Where we headed?" Damien says.

"Atlantic City. We're staying in a suite overnight. The ladies will all be at your house for a girl's sleepover." Mikael says.

Damien says to me, "Are you sure you're okay with this?"

"Yes, of course. I trust Lexi to take care of things until we get back tomorrow. This trip will do me some good," I respond.

We start our adventure at the casino, stopping at a blackjack table and play a few hands, then head off to the Hard Rock Cafe for dinner. After dinner, one of the pit bosses takes us to a private room, with a poker table on one side and a regular table on the other.

Dean hired a stripper for Damien. While she danced, I let my mind wander to Mel and how I wish I was watching her dance for me. After she's done, we move to the poker table and play an elimination Texas Hold 'Em tournament. It got down to Andy and me, and I finished him with four tens. Speaking of tens, I think to myself, Mel is definitely a ten. Actually, more like one million.

"Damn, man, didn't know you played," Damien says. "Lexi does too."

"Maybe we need a tournament with all of us when we get home." Dean says.

We play a couple more tournaments and I win them all. Around two in the morning, the pit boss comes in and lets us know they need to close the room. We head out of the casino and I walk toward the elevator.

"Our night is far from over." Mikael says.

"Where to now?" Damien asks..

"We have a VIP table at Daer. When I brought Hannah here, the bouncer recognized me, and let me know if I ever came back to let him know," Mikael says.

We head to the club. Mikael sends a text when we get there, and we're quickly escorted inside by the owner. He takes us to a reserved table down front and brings us a variety of craft beers to try. We've been there for about half an hour when the owner walks onto the stage and grabs a microphone.

"We have a very special treat for everyone tonight. Welcome to the stage Stardust."

"Thanks for having us tonight. We're here in Atlantic City tonight to celebrate our friend's upcoming wedding. Damien, get your ass up here. You too, Judd!" Dean says.

"Is this cool?" Damien asks.

"Of course, let's go," I say.

Damien joins them for a couple of songs, then Dean addresses the crowd again. "Time to slow it down for all you lovers out there."

Before they start, I call Dean over and ask him if I can sing one. Addressing the crowd, Dean says, "We have a very special treat for you now. Making his debut, Judd Walker."

Dean walks over and stands with Damien side-stage. The band plays Whitesnake's *Is This Love*.

I grab the microphone and say, "This one's for Mel."

The guys do a few more covers, and then we all head back to our table. Nobody wants to address the elephant in the room, so we just keep drinking until all the beer is gone. We decide to head back to the suite, as it's now almost five. We all sleep until Dean's cell rings around 11 to let him know the limo's downstairs. We check out and head down to the limo.

"Um, can I ask a favor, guys?" I ask.

They all nod.

"Could nobody mention to any of the girls what I said at the club?"

They agree and nobody mentions it again. We pull up to Damien's house and all the cars are still in the driveway. It's almost noon, so I can only imagine the night these ladies had. We walk down to the basement and all six of them are sound asleep. Damien sees the video camera setup, so he grabs it and connects it to the TV upstairs. The ladies' antics have us all laughing until the part where Mel says, "I want you, Judd."

"Holy shit, man," Damien exclaims.

"Dude, why are you still sitting here?" Dean says. Mikael, Andy, and Johnny nod.

"Go get her," Damien goads.

"She's just drunk. It means nothing."

"Come on, man," Damien presses.

"Look, leave it the fuck alone."

Damien clears his throat before changing the subject. "Well, I don't know about you dudes, but the stripper conga line was the highlight for me! I guess we should go wake them up."

"Before we do, I need to say something," I say. "You've all been polite enough not to mention last night and what you just heard, and I thank you. It's true, I do like Mel, but please know, I'm just not the right man for her, or anyone."

"What the fuck are you talking about?" Dean asks.

"Yeah. You have a home, a job, you're a decent dude, so why would you think that?" Damien adds.

"None of you has any idea what my life was like before I moved here. Trust me, Mel is too good for an asshole like me."

"Whatever, man, but if it were me, I'd go for it," Mikael says, as we head down to the basement. Damien cranks up an amp and plays a couple of chords. The ladies are not amused. After we get them fed, the other guys take their wives home, leaving just Mel, Damien, Lexi, and me. Mel hasn't said a word and she won't look at me.

"Judd and I are going to get you home, Mel." Damien says.

"I don't want to be alone." Mel cries.

Lexi moves closer and puts her arm around her friend while Damien and I go stand by the bar

"Talk to me, girl." Lexi says.

Mel looks at me, then says, "I'm so lonely, and I can't stand it. It sucks when you're damaged goods and no man will have you."

How can this goddess think she has nothing to offer? And she's definitely wrong about no man wanting her. I want her more than I've ever wanted anything or anyone. Every part of me wants to run over there and take her into my arms.

"For what feels like the hundredth time since we've been friends, I'm telling you, you're not damaged goods. You have a lot to offer and a woman is more than just that one particular thing. You're smart, funny, beautiful, and the best friend a girl could hope for," Lexi says.

What particular thing? I sit and stare at Mel. It hurts me down to my core seeing a woman like this. Women are amazing creatures and should be revered. I've seen firsthand what happens when men don't feel that way. Mel asks Lexi if she can shower before she goes, and of course, all I can picture is being in there with her. While the ladies head upstairs, I stay in the basement and help Damien clean up.

"What do you think Mel meant by damaged goods?" I ask.

"I'm not sure, but Lexi seems to know," Damien says.

"I hate hearing her talk like that," I say. "I guess I don't need to tell you I've had some feelings."

"Then why not ask her out?" I blurt out.

"I just can't. She deserves better. And please, don't ask me to explain."

"Got it. Just think about it, though. You heard what she said on the tape."

"I'll still take her to the Halloween party, but that has to be it and only as friends."

After helping Damien carry all the dishes upstairs, I head back to my ranch before Mel comes down. I spend the next few weeks focusing on work and fighting the temptation to call Mel. The night before the Halloween party, I'm sitting out back looking up at the stars, again thinking about my mother. My eyes fill up, the ache of missing her especially strong tonight. Without warning, her beautiful face and soothing voice are replaced by my father. Didn't I tell you, cowboys don't cry. Grow the fuck up and be a man for once. Shaking my head, I wipe my eyes and head inside.

The night of the Halloween party finally arrives, so I text Mel to let her know what time I'm coming. We dressed as Samantha and Darren from Bewitched. I get dressed in a navy blue suit, light blue shirt and a striped tie, along with my favorite well-worn tan cowboy boots with the gold decorative pattern.

On my way, I stop at a florist and buy a dozen roses. When I pull into Mel's driveway, I take a deep breath, grab the flowers and knock on her front door. A minute later, the door opens, and I almost drop the flowers. Holy fucking shit! I don't know what's sexiest, the low-cut black lace dress, her black knee-high boots, or the dark red color of the lips that I wish were wrapped around my dick.

"Um, these are for you," I say, thrusting the flowers at her.

"Thank you, they're beautiful," Mel says with a smile that makes my heart skip a beat, not to mention the effect it has on my dick. If I don't get inside her soon, I'm going to burst into flames.

"Not nearly as beautiful as you."

"You need your eyes checked."

"I'm serious. You're stunning. Shall we?" I ask, holding out my arm.

Mel hesitates for a second, then links her arm through mine. I help her up into my truck and we drive to the club. Every chance I get, I steal a glance at the gorgeous creature sitting next to me. Her dress shows me just enough of her cleavage that my mouth waters.

We pull into the parking lot and head inside. All eyes are on my date as we walk over to the table where Damien and Lexi are sitting, dressed as Danny and Sandy from Grease. After we enjoy some food and beer, Lexi and Damien entertain the crowd with a cover of You're the One That I Want.

The club's DJ, Scott, opens up the dance floor, kicking things off with Bad Company's *Feel Like Makin' Love*. Taking Mel into my arms and feeling her close to me makes me weak in the knees. Holding her tight, I inhale the scent of her coconut shampoo. It's taking every ounce of willpower not to take her mouth and make it mine.

"I love your dress," I whisper in her ear.

Blushing, she whispers, "Thank you. You look great."

We spend the rest of the night dancing. This amazing woman feels perfect in my arms, but I hate that there's clothing separating us. We hear the DJ announce the last dance, and if possible, I pull Mel even closer, hating that our night is about to end.

"I don't wanna be alone tonight," she whispers in my ear.

CHAPTER 2

Mel

W hat did you say?" Judd asks, a shocked look on his face.

"I'm sorry," I say, my cheeks heating.

"I don't want to be alone either. Please, Mel, come home with me."

"Yes." That's as much as I can muster. Am I really doing this? Who am I right now? I know this can't go anywhere, but dammit, I'm horny as hell, and I need to get fucked. Judd races back to his house so we can get inside before anyone sees me.

"Your living room is gorgeous," I say.

"Thank you. The stone fireplace is my favorite part," Judd says.

"I love this couch. The U-shape gives you plenty of room to stretch out. And the light brown works well with the cream-colored walls."

"Most of my couch time is spent reading. I bought this big TV, but I rarely watch it."

"I prefer reading too. Especially outside. Some days, I wish my job didn't have me cooped up in an office all day."

"Since you prefer reading, come with me."

Judd leads me through the arched doorway on the far side of the living room. My jaw drops when he turns the light on.

"Oh, wow, that wall is amazing. I've never seen that many books outside of a library," I say.

"As a small child, my mother turned me onto reading and I never stopped," Judd says, a sad look appearing in his gorgeous green eyes.

"I would love to meet her."

"I'm afraid that's not possible. She passed away when I was seven."

"Oh, Judd, I'm so sorry. May I ask what happened?"

"I've never told anyone. I promise when I'm ready, I will."

"I understand."

"Back to the books. When I moved in, there was nothing on that wall, so I built the shelves myself."

"I would never leave this room. I love the reading nook on the side wall."

"You're welcome anytime. Let's head back to the living room," Judd says.

"I had a lot of fun tonight," I say. "Dancing with you felt amazing."

Judd smiles and pulls me into his arms, holding me tight against him. I look up at him, and he lowers his head. Before I even realize what's happening, his lips are on mine. He eagerly explores my mouth with his tongue.

"Mmmm," I moan as I intertwine my tongue with his. A heat like nothing I've ever felt courses through my veins.

"I need to be naked with you," Judd says.

"I need that, too. Take me to bed." What the hell did I just say? Judd scoops me up and carries me to his bedroom.

"Another beautiful room," I say.

"It just got a million times more beautiful," he says, as he puts me down.

He walks behind me and I feel him unzip my dress, letting it fall to the floor.

"You're even more stunning than I imagined. You deserve to be worshiped," Judd says.

My face catches fire as I realize I'm standing here in nothing but a bra, thong, and thigh-highs. Judd runs his tongue down my spine, sending chills through my body and leaving me unable to speak.

His hands knead my ass, leaving me dripping wet. He lightly teases my clit with his thumb, causing me to suck in my breath. I'm about to kick my shoes off when Judd stops me.

"Leave those sexy heels on. Now, turn and face me, sweetheart."

I turn and see Judd on his knees. Damn, this man is naughty.

"Come to me, woman."

I move closer, my heart threatening to beat clear out of my chest. Hooking his thumbs under my thong, he pulls it down and I step out of it.

"Take that bra off. Now! I need to see those luscious breasts."

I remove my bra and toss it on the floor.

"Good girl. Now, spread those legs and hold on to my shoulders."

I grab his broad shoulders as his huge hands grab my naked ass. He leans his head between my legs and I feel his tongue swipe my pussy. My legs turn to jelly as he keeps licking me.

"You taste so fuckin' good, sweetheart."

"Mmm, feels so good," I moan.

He stops and stands, leaving me aching for more. Without a word, he scoops me up and lays me down on the black comforter covering his king-sized bed. I can only imagine what else of him is king-sized, a grin spreading across my face.

"My sweetheart, what is that naughty smile?" Judd asks.

"Oh, nothing," I say, blushing.

"I don't believe you. Tell me or no more pleasure."

"I was wondering how big your dick is." Did that just come out of my mouth? What the hell is this man doing to me?

"You'll find out soon enough. But, now, get those legs spread wide. I need to see that sweet pussy."

Given my position as a CFO, I'm used to being the boss. I like this change in pace. Plus, this is a hell of a lot more fun than work.

Judd lowers his mouth and sucks on my pussy, erasing any thoughts of work from my head.

"Oh, Judd, so good. Please don't stop."

He sucks my clit hard as he slides his fingers inside me. Nobody's ever made me feel like this. My body shakes from head to toe as I succumb to his pleasure.

"Oh, fuck, Judd. So fuckin' good."

"Such naughty words from such a pretty mouth. Now, I want you to strip me, and I damn well better enjoy it," he commands.

Judd stands at the side of his bed, so I sit up and face him. As I unbutton his shirt, I run my fingers down the light brown hair covering his muscular chest.

As I remove his belt and unfasten his pants, my breath catches in my chest. I can't wait to see what's inside those pants. Running my hands over his muscular ass, I slide his pants down. My jaw drops when I look at his black briefs.

"You're going to have to open a lot wider," Judd says.

Oh, so he wants to be like that, huh? "Please. I can handle that."

I sound more confident than I feel. His dick is one of the biggest I've ever seen. Sliding his underwear down, I come face to face, actually face to dick, with the part of his body I've thought most about.

"I can't wait to taste you," I say. After licking the pre-cum off the head, I lean forward and wrap my mouth around his dick, taking him all the way down my throat. Grabbing his muscular ass, I slide my lips up and down his erection, moaning as I suck him.

"Fuck, your mouth feels like heaven. Faster, baby," he commands. "I need to come in your mouth."

"Mmmm," I moan as I suck faster.

I fondle his balls while I get him off.

"Fuck, you're incredible," he growls, as I feel his warm cum slide down my throat. "Dance with me."

He pulls me close, and holy shit, the way his naked skin feels against mine. As we're swaying together, I say, "Damn, you taste so good. I can't wait to feel that cock inside me."

"Your wish is my command. See that bar?" he asks, pointing at the wall across from the bed.

"Yes."

"Face the wall and hold on tight. I'm gonna fuck that sweet pussy from behind."

"Please. I want you so damn bad."

I feel his massive presence behind me, and my chest heaves with desire. He spreads my legs, grabs my hips, and with one hard thrust, he's all the way in. And holy fucking shit, I've never felt anything like this. I hold the bar so tight, my knuckles turn white as he pounds into me. The sound of his balls slapping my ass as he fucks me is the hottest thing I've ever heard.

"Fuck, woman, your pussy feels incredible."

"Mmmm, feels so good," I moan.

"Come for me, sweetheart. Drench my cock."

"Fuck me harder," I cry out.

Judd growls as he pounds me harder and faster until my body quakes and a tidal wave soaks his dick. He doesn't stop pounding my pussy and I explode over and over. The bar is the only thing holding me up. I feel him shoot a massive load inside me.

He scoops me up and lays me down on his bed.

"Get those legs open as wide as you can." He slides his hands under my ass and lifts my ass off the bed. His mouth covers my mound, and he sucks hard. I'm so sensitive, I can barely take it. Writhing, I scream as his tongue sends me soaring, waves of pleasure coursing through my body.

"Fuck, you taste so good."

He blankets my body with his incredible muscles as again I get to take his dick inside me. He's different this time. Holding me close, his thrusts are still deep, but his pace is slower. My nails rake over his muscular back as we fuck again and again until there's nothing left.

Lying next to this sexy cowboy, completely drenched in a variety of fluids, is like something out of a steamy romance novel.

"I never knew sex could feel like that," I whisper.

"Me either, my beautiful goddess."

Judd kisses my forehead as he pulls me close. I could definitely get used to feeling his arms around me.

"Did I mention that I really liked your dress?" Judd asks, laughing.

"You don't say? I couldn't tell," I tease.

A yawn escapes my lips. Judd pulls the covers over us and turns off the light. I fall asleep to the sound of his breathing.

Monday morning arrives way too soon. I'm sitting in my office staring at my computer screen. Focusing on anything other than Judd is proving futile. I think back to the morning after. We ate a quiet breakfast together, then he took me home, leaving me with only a cordial goodbye. I guess he regrets sleeping with me, and I shouldn't have expected any other outcome.

A familiar male voice snaps me out of my reverie. "Good morning, Sunshine. How was your weekend?"

Jason Donnelly has the office next to mine and we're on the executive board together, along with being friends and confidants.

"Good morning. Just a normal weekend," I respond.

"Like hell. You had sex," he says.

"I did not!"

"Again, like hell. I can tell that a mile away. Who was he?"

"First, you have to promise me this stays right here."

"Of course."

"You know my friend Lexi? He's her next-door neighbor. He's a real-life cowboy and his name is Judd."

"Damn, girl. Gives a whole new meaning to a certain Big and Rich song."

"Oh, ha, ha, ha."

"Seriously, though, you deserve this."

"I'm not so sure."

"Don't make me yell at you. I don't give a shit what Trish and the rest of your family say. You're amazing and you deserve to be loved."

Just as I'm about to respond, our boss, Mr. O'Laughlin, appears in my doorway with another man who likes to be around my age. Mr. O'Laughlin is close to retirement age, so I can't help but wonder if this other man is his future replacement.

"Good morning to you both," Mr. O'Laughlin says. "Allow me to introduce my nephew, Daniel. Daniel, please meet our Chief Information Officer Jason Donnelly and our Chief Financial Office, Melissa McNeill."

"Pleased to meet you," I say.

"Good morning," Jason says.

Daniel sneers at us, but doesn't utter a word.

"Board meeting at ten," Mr. O'Laughlin says as he's walking away.

"Well, he's a shithead," Jason says.

"I was going to say dickhead, but yours works too," I say. "Wanna join me for some coffee and a quick bite before the meeting?"

"Yep. Let me just put my stuff down."

After grabbing my coffee and bagel, I head back to my office and hear my cell. Lexi.

"Hello," I say.

"Spill it, girl," Lexi says.

"Spill what?"

"You know what, Judd."

"There's nothing to spill."

"You mean nothing happened after you left the club?"

"He took me home." She doesn't need to know it was the next morning.

"Bummer. I bet he's good in the sack."

"I wouldn't know." Liar. Good is a damn understatement. I want more than anything to tell my best friend what he did to me, but not until we figure out what this thing is.

"Maybe someday. The other reason I called is to remind you about Damien's birthday in a couple of weeks. The party will be at our house."

"Of course I'll be there. I wouldn't miss it."

"Thanks, girl. I'll call you later."

"Talk later. Love you."

"Love you more."

Jason appears in my doorway. "Ready to head into the boardroom?"

"Nope," I laugh, grabbing my coffee cup.

"So, forgive me for being nosy, but why didn't you tell Lexi?"

"I really want to, but she's such a romantic that she would be bugging me daily to find out what exactly was going on with Judd, and I'm just not ready for that. So far, it's looking like just a one-night stand."

"Gotcha. Just be careful. You wouldn't want her to find out you were keeping something from her."

"I know. I just need to see how this goes first. But, for right now, I need to focus on staying awake for the meeting," I joke.

"We should get more coffee," Jason says, laughing.

The meeting ends up being not as bad as I thought, though a few times my mind wandered to a certain sexy cowboy. And now, my side is sore from Jason's elbow. The rest of the day goes much faster. Most people look forward to the end of the workday, but I hate the thought of going home alone.

I would love to see Judd again, but he hasn't called or texted, so I don't want to seem pushy. A couple more weeks go by with not so much as one word from him. The day of Damien's birthday party is here, and I'm completely freaked out by the thought of seeing Judd. I grab my favorite jeans and a low-cut black t-shirt.

After we surprise Damien with pictures of key moments in his relationship with Lexi, we eat, then start a poker tournament. We're all laughing and chatting. All of us except Lexi and Judd, who are taking this way too seriously. One by one, the poker king and queen pick the rest of us off. Judd makes a fatal error and calls with a cursed hand, and Lexi takes the win.

After the party, I'm sitting in my car when my phone beeps. A text from Judd.

Judd: It was great to see you.

Me: Great to see you too.

Judd: You looked beautiful.

Me: Thanks, handsome.

Judd: Have a good night.

Me: You too.

That's it? Have a good night. He fucks me senseless, ghosts me, and that's all he has to say. That tells me everything I need to know. This was a one-night stand and nothing more. Tears stream down my face as I drive home. Just once I want someone to love me. Not use me, try to get money from me, or anything else. Just fucking love me. I barely held it together when Lexi invited everyone for Thanksgiving. But, as usual, since I won't give my sister money, I'm uninvited to the family dinner.

After stopping at the park to compose myself, I finish my drive home. My eyes go wide when I see a pickup truck parked in my driveway.

"What are you doing here?" I ask.

CHAPTER 3

Judd

"I needed to see you," I say.

"Well, now you've seen me," she says, frowning.

"Please don't be like that."

"So, I shouldn't be mad that you ghosted me?"

"I know I was an asshole."

"Yeah, actually you were, but that's all I deserve."

"Why do you say that?"

"Nevermind."

"Talk to me, Mel."

"Nothing to talk about."

"Come on, sweetheart, I know something's bothering you."

"Yeah, being ignored by someone who I thought might actually like me."

"I do like you, and I think we can be great friends."

"I get it, and honestly, I could use another friend. I love Lexi, but she's not around as much now that she's with Damien."

"I don't see as much of Damien either."

"Well, thank you for stopping by," Mel says.

"Of course. Good night."

"Good night."

That couldn't have gone worse. I wait for Mel to get inside before I get back in my truck. After sitting and changing my mind a million times, I finally leave, but damn, I wanted to knock on her door and kiss her. If only.

Other than a few phone calls, I've had little contact with Mel, but I'll see her later at Damien and Lexi's for Thanksgiving. I get to their house first. Lexi smiles when I hand her a bouquet. We all hang out in the living room while Mel helps Lexi. I keep stealing glances at Mel. She looks especially beautiful in a chocolate brown tee shirt and jeans.

After we all leave, I wait for Mel to get to her car and text her.

Me: Join for a cup of coffee?

Mel: Okay. Where?

Me: IHOP

Mel: Sounds good.

After she pulls out of the driveway, I get in my truck and follow her. After we order our coffee, an awkward silence fills the air. Tensing up, I say, "I want to take you on a date."

"Really?" Mel asks.

"You seem surprised."

"After not hearing from you, I am."

"I'm sorry."

"That's it? I give myself to you and that's all I get?"

"I know this isn't an excuse, but I got scared."

"Scared of me?"

"No. My past."

"I'm a good listener."

"I've never told anyone why I left Texas."

"I don't want to push..."

"Do you promise not to judge me until I finish?"

"You have my word."

"One other request."

"What?"

"I don't want to do this here."

"How about my house? That way, Damien and Lexi don't see me at yours."

"Thanks, Mel."

"My pleasure."

Mel's face looks like a woman who just got the gift she'd always wanted. My heart skips a beat as I watch her sip her hazelnut-scented coffee. After polishing off an entire pot, we head out. We're sitting on Mel's couch. Trying to avoid continuing our conversation, I look around her living room.

"I love the color you painted the room," I say.

"Thanks. Lilac is one of my favorite colors. I like the way it looks with the stone fireplace."

"It does."

"My favorite piece is my couch. I love the charcoal color, not to mention how comfortable it is."

"I also noticed the shelf with the horses. Do you ride?"

"When I was a kid. My dad rented a stable and bought me a horse, a beautiful golden palomino that I named Dolly. Then, when the drugs took over, and he needed money, she was the first thing he sold. I was devastated. The picture next to the figurines is her."

"I'm so sorry. So, um, I guess I can't avoid the subject at hand any longer."

"Please don't feel pressured."

"Thanks, but honestly, I need to do this."

Mel lays a hand on my arm, but says nothing.

"When I was only seven years old, I lost my mom."

"Oh my god, that's awful. What happened?" Mel asks. I see tears slide down her cheeks.

"My mom, Joanna, was one of those special people. She was a housewife and always waiting with a delicious homemade baked good when I got home from school."

"She sounds amazing."

"She was. You should have seen her, tall and slender, with light brown hair and eyes to match. She was also intelligent and pushed me to earn good grades. Mom graduated from college Magna Cum Laude with a degree in criminal justice. She had her pick of law schools, but she chose marriage and a child."

"I wish I could have met her."

"She would have loved you."

"Can I ask what happened?"

"When I got home from school, I knew something was wrong when there was nothing in the oven. My dad and his rancher buddies were sitting around the kitchen. I can still remember his exact words."

"What did he say?"

"Your mom had a heart attack today while she was getting dinner ready. When I asked if she would be okay, he told me she wouldn't be coming home."

Tears threaten to spill over as I remember that day vividly. I look at Mel and her face crumbles.

"Oh, Judd, I don't know what to say."

"I wish that were the end of the story, but no. Graduating high school at the top of my class, I had my pick of colleges, but I had to put that dream on hold to help my dad. One afternoon, I was working in the barn. Dad asked me to clean the loft and as I was raking out fresh hay, the rake caught a loose floorboard and lifted it. I looked inside and saw a black steel security box with the keys still in it. After sitting down, I opened the box and saw a knife covered in dried blood."

"Oh my god, I'm almost afraid to hear more."

"Under the knife, in a plastic sandwich bag, I saw a note from my mom telling my dad she was leaving him. The realization of what happened hit me like a tidal wave. An anger like none I'd ever felt coursed through my veins. My father killed my beloved mother and his friends were helping him cover it up. I hid the box in my jacket and ran to my truck. I knew what I had to do, but I also knew what the consequences would be. My dad and his fellow ranchers were a tight-knit community with their own unwritten code. Any man who dared break that code might as well just leave town."

Mel sniffles as I keep talking. It's as if she can feel the way my chest tightens as I think about my mom.

"The following afternoon, Dad and I were working in the stables when we heard a car pull up. We walked outside and the town sheriff was standing there with one of his deputies to arrest my dad. The news of his arrest spread like wildfire. Word that it was me who turned Dad in also spread. I couldn't enter a single business in town without glares and angry whispers. Fucking bunch of assholes thought what I did was worse," I shout as blind rage courses through my body.

"So, that's why you moved here?"

"Yeah. Well, that and well, there's one more thing I need to tell you."

"What?"

"I was engaged. The daughter of one of my dad's rancher buddies."

Mel stares at me, not saying a word. Fear spreads through me. Did I just ruin this by telling her that last part? She finally speaks and I breathe a sigh of relief.

"And you've kept this in all these years?"

"I almost told Damien, but I just couldn't bring myself to."

"But you told me?"

"Yeah. There's just something about you."

She nestles herself against me, laying her head on my shoulder. I feel my eyes filling up and I try to stop it before Mel sees. I fail.

"I'm sorry," I whisper.

"For what?"

I point at my eyes. "My dad told me at the funeral that cowboys don't cry."

"Well, he was wrong. You need that release sometimes," Mel says, as she caresses my cheek.

That's all it takes and my eyes spill over. She wraps her arms around me and holds tight. Burying my head into her shoulder, I soak her shirt. Looking up, my eyes meet hers and I lose all control. Putting my hand on the back of her head, I pull her towards me and crush my lips to hers. She opens for me and I slide my tongue into her mouth, making her moan. Holding each other tight, we share the longest kiss I've ever experienced.

"Stay with me tonight, please. I don't wanna be alone," Mel begs.

"Neither do I."

When we get to her bedroom, we undress and climb into her beautiful queen-sized canopy bed. The plum-colored satin sheets feel good against my skin, but not nearly as good as this sexy goddess.

"Do you want to talk more?" Mel asks.

"Later, but right now, I need to be inside you."

"Mmmm, please, baby. I want you."

"Get that sexy ass on top of me, baby," I say.

She straddles me and grabs my dick. She lowers herself down the full length of my erection, and fuck, she feels so good. I wrap my arms around her and pull her tight against me.

"Oh, Judd, I love the way you feel inside me."

"Sweetheart, you feel like the sweetest heaven."

Her breathing shallows and her moans intensify until I feel her body shake. She unleashes a string of dirty words that would make a sailor blush. Keeping my dick inside of her, I roll her onto her back and thrust into her, until I empty inside her.

We're laying in each other's arms when she says, "Thank you for trusting me with your secret. I can't even imagine what that was like."

"Thanks for listening."

"My pleasure," she says with a wink.

"I get a feeling you have some things you've been hiding, too."

"How could you tell?"

"Been there. I could tell by things you said."

"There are things I've never even told Lexi."

"When you're ready, I'm here."

"Thank you."

Mel lays her head on my chest and I hear light snores, the cutest sound I've ever heard. We're enjoying breakfast the following morning. Mel's dressed for work, and holy shit, am I having fantasies looking at her dressed in her business suit.

"So, do you have plans tonight?" I ask her.

"Nope, I'm boring!"

"The hell you are! Would you care to join me for karaoke? I found a bar about an hour outside of town, The Full Moon Saloon. I go there when I want to be alone."

"I've seen pictures of that place and always wanted to go. I'm usually home by five."

"Is six good for me to pick you up?"

"Yes, that works."

After helping Mel clean up, she leaves for work, so I head back to my ranch to get some work done. All I can think about is taking her out tonight. I'm so lost in thought that I nearly jump out of my skin when I hear a voice.

"Hey, Judd. Sorry I startled you."

"Hey, Damien."

"You looked lost in thought. Everything okay?"

"Yeah, all good. Gotta get back to work."

I race off before he has time to respond. Heading into my stables, I check on my horses, stopping to chat with Rex.

"Hey buddy. I think I might have finally found her," I say.

Rex nudges me with his snout.

"I just wish I was enough for her. But I'll enjoy her company as long as I can," I say as I pet Rex's head.

Looking up at the loft, I picture being up there having sex with Mel. An actual roll in the hay. I chuckle. After I finish my work, I get ready and head out, stopping at a florist on the way. Red roses in hand, I ring Mel's doorbell and go weak in the knees when I see her in tight jeans, cowgirl boots and a low-cut white tee-shirt covered with a purple cardigan.

"Please come in," she says with a smile.

Handing her the bouquet, I say, "Wow! You look beautiful."

"Thank you," she says with a giggle. My dick stirs.

I watch as she puts the flowers in the water. All I want to do is grab her and kiss her. Instead, I walk over and hold out my arm for her. She links her arm through mine, and we walk out to my truck. As we're driving to the saloon, I say, "So, would you like to sing a duet with me tonight?"

"Um, I'm not sure I'd be any good."

"It's not about being good, it's about having fun."

"Oh, what the hell! I'm in."

"I can't wait to sing with you. Now, what do you think we should do?"

"I have a favorite rock duet, if that works?"

"I love rock. What song?"

"Ozzy and Lita Ford's *If I Close My Eyes Forever*."

"Perfect."

When we get to the saloon, we grab an empty table. Mel waits while I sign us up for karaoke, as well as order drinks and food.

"I ordered you a glass of Moscato," I say.

"How'd you know that was my favorite?"

"I saw a bottle in your fridge."

"You're so thoughtful."

"My pleasure, darlin'," Judd says.

"I love how they made this look like an old saloon."

"That's one of my favorite things about coming here."

"This is more my speed. I'm happy for Lexi, but her club just isn't my cup of tea."

"I know what you mean. I was mostly goin' on the group outings just to see you."

Mel blushes as she smiles. She truly is the most beautiful woman I've ever seen. When Mel's wine and my beer arrive, I hold up my glass. "To us."

"Cheers," Mel says and we clink glasses.

After we finish eating, we wait for karaoke to start.

"Would you like to dance?" I ask.

"I'd love to."

Taking her hand, we walk to the dance floor. I take her into my arms and she buries her head into my chest. We sway to the music, and I'm completely lost in her. The scent of her lilac shampoo is intoxicating, and I breathe her in. She looks up at me, her eyes shining like the brightest sapphires. Lowering my head, I kiss her and my stomach flutters. When the song ends, the DJ announces that karaoke will start soon, so we wait until we're called to the stage.

When our turn comes up, we walk onto the stage and I pull up our song. When Mel opens her mouth, the sound that comes out is like nothing I've ever heard. She has an alto voice with a small amount of rasp and she's incredible. When our song is done, everyone stands and cheers. I even hear a few people yelling encore. I look over at Mel, and she has a huge smile on her face.

When we're back at our table, I say, "Wow, you have a beautiful voice."

"Thank you. You're also an amazing singer," she says.

"And you were worried."

"I've been told before that I wasn't good at anything."

"Oh, sweetheart, whoever told you that is an ass."

"You're so sweet."

We stay about another hour, heading out, when I see Mel yawn. I pull into her driveway and walk her to her door.

"I had a great time tonight," I say.

"Me too. Thank you for a great evening," Mel says.

"I'd love to do it again."

"I would too."

"Maybe this weekend?"

"Sounds good."

"I'll call you. Good night, Mel."

"Good night, Judd."

CHAPTER 4
Mel

Sitting in my office the following morning, I'm daydreaming about my date last night when Jason appears in my doorway.

"Girl! You've been holding out on me," he says.

"How so?"

"A friend of mine was at The Full Moon last night and sent me a video of an amazing karaoke duet."

"Oh, yeah?"

"I had no idea you could sing."

"Neither did I. Judd talked me into it."

"Well, you need to do that more often. And damn, that dude is crazy about you!"

"No, he's not."

"Trust me, he is. Watch this."

Jason walks over and pulls up the video on his phone. Judd's eyes don't leave me through the entire performance. All of my attention was on singing and I never noticed. Is it possible? Could a man actually love me? Not if you ask my family, but maybe they're wrong.

"So, now can you please tell your family to fuck off?" Jason says, as if he was reading my mind.

"I wish I could."

"Seriously, girl, why can't you?"

"It wouldn't be right."

"And the way they treat you is? What does Judd think about it?"

"Haven't told him yet."

"Why not?"

"He went through hell as a kid. I couldn't burden him with my stuff, too. Besides, what if he thinks I'm too much drama?"

"Honey, he won't think that. But you should tell him."

"I guess."

"I gotta run, meeting this morning. Wanna grab lunch later?"

"Sounds good. My schedule is open today, so yell when you're ready."

I'm working on year-end expense reports when my assistant Allie appears, a vase of yellow roses with red tips in her hands.

"These just came for you," Allie says.

I walk over and take the vase from her. "Thank you."

Putting the vase down, I open the card.

To the most beautiful woman in the world.

Judd

Knowing that different colors have different meanings, I look up a rose color chart. Yellow roses with red tips signify friendship and falling in love. Tears fill my eyes. Is this sweet, sexy man falling in love with me, or is he trying to tell me he just wants to be friends? By the time Jason comes down, I'm in full freakout mode.

"Beautiful flowers. And might they be from the cowboy?" Jason says.

"They are and I'm a wreck."

"Why?"

"The color he picked can mean either friendship or falling in love."

"And?"

"If he only wants friendship, I'll be disappointed, but the thought of him falling in love with me scares the hell out of me."

Jason walks over to me and puts his hands on my shoulders. "Take a couple of deep breaths and calm down."

I feel a little better after I take Jason's advice. "Thanks."

"My advice, if you want it, is to just let things happen naturally."

"Things have been great the way they are so far, so you're right."

"That's my girl. Now, let's go get lunch."

The rest of the day dragged on. These damn reports are boring as hell. Just as I'm dragging my sorry ass through the front door, my cell rings. I smile when I see Judd's name appear.

"Well, hello there, cowboy. Thanks for the beautiful roses," I say.

"My pleasure ma'am."

I hate being called ma'am, yet when Judd does it, my entire body gets warm, especially on one particular part.

"So, what's up?"

"Thought you might want some company for dinner. I could grab some Italian and come over."

"I'd love that."

"What would you like to eat?"

Your dick. "Stuffed shells are my favorite."

"Sounds great. I'll be there in about an hour. And please, leave your work outfit on."

"Can't wait."

Why did he want me to leave the outfit on? I hope it involves something dirty, like maybe he has a fantasy about a woman in power. To test my theory, I pull my hair up into a bun and leave my glasses on. Just thinking about it has my body on fire. When my doorbell rings, I race to the door. Judd's standing there with a bag of food.

"Good evening, sweetheart," he says and my insides turn to goo.

"Good evening," I say with a curtsy. Judd laughs, something he rarely does, and something I need to hear more of. "Please come in."

He bows, then places the bag on my kitchen table. I feel at ease around him, and it's a pleasant feeling for a change.

"Let me grab plates. What would you like to drink?" I ask.

"Beer, if you have it."

"Of course."

I grab a beer for Judd and a wine cooler for myself. After grabbing plates and silverware, we sit down to eat. After dinner, Judd insists on cleaning the dishes.

"Keep that up and I'll never let you leave," I joke.

"I wouldn't complain," he says, flashing me the smile that drives me wild. "Now, might we move to your living room?"

"Of course."

We sit down together on my couch. He caresses my cheek and says, "You look so damn sexy."

"Thanks. Why did you want me to keep this on?"

"Because I'm the boss and I said so. Where's your home office?"

"Right through there," I say, pointing at the door.

Judd walks to the office and I follow him. Once we're inside, he says, "I wanna see you bent over the desk. Now!"

Holy shit! I walk over, face the desk and bend over, resting my arms on the desk. Judd walks up behind me and grabs my hips. He grinds into my ass, and I can feel his erection straining against his jeans. He slides my skirt up, revealing my thong and my thigh-high, sheer black stockings. He hooks his thumbs under the band of my thong and slides it off.

"That sexy little ass is begging for my hand."

"Please, Judd. Spank me. I've been a naughty girl."

He sits down in the chair across from my desk.

"Get your ass over here and lay across my lap."

His hand swats my left ass cheek and the sweet sting has my pussy aching. He repeats the same on my right cheek and I moan.

"Fuck, I want you so bad," I say.

"Did I say you could speak, naughty girl?" he says and swats both cheeks again and I can barely hold it together. I need his cock so damn bad I can taste it.

"Mmmm, look at that ass, red from my hand. You're so fucking hot, my dirty little sex goddess. Now get that ass up and strip for me. And make sure I enjoy the show."

Fuck, I love this side of him. I remove my jacket and unbutton my blouse, revealing my black lace bra. After removing my bra, I run my hands down my naked breasts and lick my lips. He opens his jeans as he watches me and I see he's not wearing underwear.

"Mmm, good, baby," he moans, taking his dick into his hand and stroking himself. "I want the stockings to stay on."

I'm about to remove my glasses when he stops me.

"No, no, leave those on. You look so damn sexy. Bend over the desk. NOW! I'm going to fuck you senseless."

I bend over the desk and look over at my sexy cowboy.

"Now, spread those legs as wide as you can," he says as he walks over and stands behind me.

My breathing shallows as I feel him against me. With one hard thrust, his cock's inside my pussy. "Oh, Judd."

"That's it. Scream my name."

"Oh, Judd. Feels so good. Mmm."

"Louder and dirtier or I stop."

"JUDD! Please pound my wet pussy with that fucking gigantic cock."

"More, baby."

"Please spank me while you pound my pussy. I wanna feel your hand and your balls slapping my ass."

"That's my naughty sweetheart."

He's fucking me so hard, my breasts are bouncing like balloons in the Macy's Thanksgiving Parade on a windy day. I'm close to exploding and when Judd's fingers find my clit, that pushes me over the edge.

"Oh, Judd, so fucking good, oh god," I scream as I drench his dick. Holy shit. As waves of pleasure ripple through me, Judd empties inside me, growling as he finishes.

"Damn, woman. That was so hot."

"That's the first time I've ever squirted. It felt incredible."

"I'm honored to be your first."

"I'm glad it was you."

Judd sits down in the chair and pats his lap, so I sit down. He pulls me close and whispers, "I wanna fall asleep with you in my arms tonight."

"I want that too."

Judd gathers up all of our clothes and carries them to my bedroom.

"Would you mind if I shower?" Judd asks.

"Not at all. I kinda made a mess all over you." We both laugh.

"Care to join me?"

"In the shower? I've, um, never showered with anyone before."

"Really?"

"I've never had a man want to."

"Wow, a goddess like you?"

"Trust me, you're the only one who thinks that."

"Then these other men need their heads examined."

My heart flutters every time he utters kind words to me. I have little experience being treated like this, and I'm not sure how to handle it, so I just smile and say, "Thanks."

"One way or another, I'm going to show you how a man should treat a woman."

"Mmm. That'll be a pleasant change."

We get in the shower and I turn the water on.

"I hate to tell you this, but I only have girly-scented stuff."

"That's okay. I don't mind smelling like you," he says with a wink.

Judd grabs my puff, squirts some gel on it, and lathers me up. I must admit, I enjoy being pampered like this, especially by such a sexy man. He washes my hair, and his fingers send chills up my spine. While I rinse off, I watch Judd wash himself and damn, seeing his hands on his dick drives me crazy.

I felt self-conscious standing naked in front of the mirror and blurt out, "I have extra toothbrushes." Way to sound like an idiot.

"Thanks," he says with a smile.

We finish up and get into bed, still naked. Judd pulls me close, and I lay my head on his chest.

"I've told you about my past," Judd says. "Now, it's your turn."

Sighing, I say, "I was afraid this day would come. This was nice while it lasted."

"What do you mean?"

"Let's just say my family leaves a lot to be desired."

"Tell me. If you want. No pressure."

"Well, it helped you to tell me, right?"

"Yeah, very much."

"Well, then I guess I'll give it a whirl."

Judd hugs me a little tighter as I start. "I'm the oldest of two girls. When I was a child, I was close to my dad. Then when I was in high school, he had an accident at work, and something changed. He got into drugs, causing my mom to leave. She took my little sister with her, but I stayed."

"Why?"

"I felt bad leaving him alone. Mom resented me for it and she's never let me forget it. But as I got closer to graduating from high school and starting college, things got worse and I had to leave. Mom wouldn't take me, so my grandparents did."

Judd says nothing, so I continue.

"I was living in an apartment after college. Then, when they retired to Florida, they sold me their house."

"This house?"

"Yep."

"My dad got so bad that I saw him at a car show and he didn't even know who I was until I told him."

"I'm sorry you went through all that."

"Oh, we've only scratched the surface. There's a lot more with my dad and I haven't gotten to my mom and my sister yet. But I'll save that for another time."

"Sounds like it's a good thing we found each other."

I smile and respond, "I think you're right."

The next morning, as I'm getting in my car to head to work, Judd says, "Maybe I need to keep some stuff here. Like a change of clothes and shower stuff."

That sets off my freakout alarm, and I just nod and say, "Have a good day."

"You as well," he says, then gets in his truck and heads home.

I yell at myself for my entire drive to work. After I put my stuff down in my office, I head right to Jason's and plop down in a chair, my head in my hands.

"What did you do?" Jason asks.

I tell him about that last conversation with Judd. "How could my response have been so stupid?"

"It wasn't stupid. You panicked. I get it."

"Come on, it was stupid."

"Honey, we all have those moments. It may have been awkward, but it certainly wasn't stupid."

"Have I told you I'm lucky to have you?"

"All the time, and I feel the same way."

"What am I gonna do about Judd?"

44

"Easy. Talk to him. Have you told him about Derek?"

"No. I started telling him some stuff about my dad, but I stopped before I got to that."

"Don't wait too long. Trust me, I would want to know early on."

I nod, but say nothing , instead making a mental note to talk to Judd tonight.

CHAPTER 5
Judd

"Well, Rex, I think I fucked up, buddy," I say as I feed him a piece of apple. Rex nuzzles me as he eats. "I may have pushed Mel too hard." This is one of those times I wish animals could talk. How am I going to fix this? I can't stand the thought of losing her, even if I don't deserve her. I'm just coming downstairs to make dinner when I hear a knock at my door. I smile when I see who's on the other side.

"Can I come in?" Mel whispers.

"Of course."

"I'm sorry about this morning."

"For what?"

"The way I reacted."

"I pushed too hard."

"No, you didn't."

"Then, what happened?"

Mel sits down on my couch and sighs. "I was married."

Married? Mel, my beautiful goddess was married? Why would she wait until now to tell me? And why does it feel like someone just put a knife through my heart?

Sitting down next to her, I say, "And it didn't go well?"

"That's the understatement of the year. I mean, things started out good. But that ended when we tried to start a family."

Tears slide down her beautiful face, breaking my heart.

"We went to a fertility specialist, and she determined I was barren. Derek was angry. He wanted kids more than anything. And I was the worthless bitch that wouldn't give them to him. His words."

"He was wrong on so many fronts."

"Was he though?"

"Yeah, he was. For one thing, it's that you couldn't, not wouldn't."

"That didn't matter. And trust me, he made sure I didn't forget. I couldn't do anything right."

"Oh, sweetheart."

"Any little thing that didn't meet his standards, he would scream and call me names. And I believed everything he said. When he served me with divorce papers, he did it at a party in front of our friends, well, his friends actually. He said I was damaged goods and no man would ever want me. And not one person did anything but laugh at me."

Her body shakes as her face crumbles. I pull her tight against me as she buries her head in my chest and soaks my shirt. An anger builds inside me. How could someone make this incredible goddess of a woman feel like this?

"Nobody's ever going to hurt you again," I whisper in her ear.

She looks up at me, her sapphire eyes dim, her face stained. "Promise?"

"Promise."

Her face brightens as she gazes at me. I lean in and claim her mouth. Fuck, I love this woman. I wrap my arms around her as I lay her back on the couch as we kiss. When I finally let her up for air, she says, "Will you read to me?"

"Really?"

"I mean, unless that's too weird,"

"No, it just surprised me. It's nice to have someone share my love of books. Wait here."

I remember that I saw a collection of Sesame Street stuff in Mel's living room, so I grab my childhood copy of The Monster at the End of This Book. She squeals when I show her the book.

"Oh my god, Grover is my favorite character, and that was my favorite book as a kid!"

"I noticed your shelf in your living room."

"You're so sweet."

"You always loved Sesame Street, huh?"

"Yeah. Besides, Grover, I also love Mr. Snuffleupagus. When I was a kid, I always thought it would be fun to ride on him. I still have my stuffed Snuffy from my childhood."

"And the rubber duck collection in your bathroom?"

"That's thanks to Ernie. I used to walk around singing *Rubber Ducky, You're the One*. I never really belonged anywhere, especially in my family. But Sesame Street helped with that and that's why the show is still so important to me."

"I love learning this stuff about you. I thought maybe the rubber ducks were a nod to my favorite childhood movie."

"What movie?"

"I was always into trucks, the big ones. There was a movie named Convoy about trucks. One of the driver's nicknames was Rubber Duck."

"Never saw that movie, but I'd love to sometime."

"I'll see if I can find it."

She smiles and kicks her shoes off then lays down, her head in my lap as I read. A few pages in and I hear the cutest little snores. Looking down at the goddess sound asleep on my couch, my heart swells. I slide out from under her, scoop her up, and carry her to my bedroom. After getting her nestled under the covers, I get ready, then climb into bed next to her. I drift off to sleep, listening to the sound of her breathing.

Mel's still asleep when I wake up the next morning. She looks like an angel, a peaceful look on her beautiful face. She stirs awake and turns to face me.

"What happened?"

"You fell asleep when I was reading to you, so I carried you to bed."

"I'm sorry. It wasn't because of you."

"I know that. You had a rough night."

"How are you so sweet?"

"Life hasn't always been kind to me, so I try to be kind to others."

"I love that. The world needs more people like you."

"Thanks, sweetheart. So, would you care to go out to breakfast, then take a walk in the park?"

"That sounds perfect. Would you mind terribly if I shower and change first?"

"Of course not. How about I pick you up in an hour?"

"I'm looking forward to it."

About an hour later, I knock on Mel's door. When she opens it, I go weak. She's dressed in blue jeans and a plum sweater, finished with a pair of cowgirl boots. My mouth waters as I stand there, gawking at her. Her cheeks turn bright red as she smiles.

"Shall we, my angel?" I ask.

"Yes, my devil," she says with a wink. I take her coat from her and help her into it.

"Why, thank you. You're such a gentleman. Well, at least outside of the bedroom," she teases.

"Only because you're so damn sexy! You drive me wild."

"Right back at ya, cowboy!"

After breakfast, we drive to the park. As we walk, I take her hand in mine and there goes that feeling in my stomach again. I know exactly what it is, and it both excites and scares me. It was easy to give her my body. My heart is another story. For now, I'll just enjoy every moment I spend with this incredible woman. We find an empty bench and sit down to do some people-watching.

I hear a commotion and look down at the playground. There's a woman with four out-of-control kids making more noise than a football stadium full of fans.

"Yikes," Mel says.

"I know a perfect way to turn them out."

"Oh yeah, what?"

I pull her close, crushing my lips to hers. I feel her tongue tangle with mine

"Well, if it isn't the world's biggest loser," a voice behind us says.

I don't recognize the voice, so I look at Mel. All the color drains from her face.

"Derek?" I whisper. Mel nods.

"Being a dick to me won't make yours bigger."

I don't even try to control my laughter.

"Yuck it up now, dipshit," Derek sneers. "You'll see."

The noisy group from the playground gets louder and I see them approaching our bench. The woman drags the kids over, an angry look on her face.

"Derek, you could help me, you know," she says.

Mel bursts out laughing. "Is that your family?"

"Yeah," Derek says.

Mel laughs so hard, she snorts and can't talk, so I jump in. "Now I understand why you came over here to insult your ex. I'd be jealous of her life if mine was a nightmare like yours." Turning to Mel, I say, "Let's go, baby."

Mel can't stop laughing the entire way out of the park, and even when we get in my truck. She takes a deep breath and can finally speak. "Thank you so much. You have no idea how much I needed that."

"I'm impressed with how you handled that."

"Thank you. I don't deserve you."

She's right, she deserves so much better. "So, since our walk got cut short, is there anything else you'd like to do today?"

"I'm not sure, but I do know I want to spend it with you."

"Well, how about we order takeout?"

"I'd actually prefer to cook."

"I thought takeout was your preference."

"That's more Lexi's thing. Even though I'm alone, I still cook almost every night."

"Well, then, how about we cook together tonight?"

"Sounds perfect."

"So, what else do you enjoy doing?"

"Well, you."

"Oh, you can bet we'll be doing that. But, what else?"

"Promise you won't tease me? I'm kinda nerdy."

"Of course."

"I love jigsaw puzzles. They keep me busy when it's too cold or rainy to be outside."

"I wish I had some."

"I have plenty, so I'll grab a couple. I was hoping to stop at my house so I can grab an overnight bag. That is, if you want me to spend the night."

"You bet I do. I promise you'll be too tired to move when I'm done with you tonight."

"Mmm, Judd," she moans and there goes my dick.

"So, what were you thinking about for dinner?" I ask.

"Chicken's my favorite. I usually just grab a breast and sauté it in Italian dressing."

Great, now all I can think about is my hands on her luscious breasts. "That sounds delicious. What would you want to have with it?"

"You like spinach?"

"Yeah. Especially sauteed. How about that, plus some oven-roasted potatoes?"

"My mouth's watering already."

She keeps up those comments, and the only place we're gonna be cooking is in bed!

After stopping at the grocery store and her house, we head back to mine. As I watch her prep the food for dinner my mind races. I can picture her living here as my wife, helping me with the animals, living this simple life together. And, of course, I picture her in my bed, taking every bit of what I give her. I can't help myself. I'm falling for this woman. Hard.

"What can I do?" I ask.

"How about peeling and cutting the potatoes? I'm a lefty and have the worst time using a peeler," she says, laughing.

"Yes ma'am."

I get to work while she finishes prepping the chicken and getting it in a pan. Watching her as she washes her hands, I can't wait to have those hands on my dick later. She rinses off the spinach and gets that into a second pan. We get the potatoes in the oven, then Mel cooks up the other food while I set the table. The food smells delicious, and it tastes even better. We clean up, then sit down on the couch.

"That was absolutely divine, just like the woman who cooked it."

"Thank you. I had fun doing that together."

"Just you wait. The fun has only just begun."

"Good, because I want you."

Fuck, this woman! She's as close to perfection as anyone could be.

"Shall we get started on one of the puzzles?"

"Um, I kinda wanna do something else right now."

Raising my eyebrows, I say, "Oh, and what might that be?"

"Please, my sexy cowboy, take me to bed."

Scooping her up, I carry her to my bedroom and set her down. "Strip for me, baby. And make it hot!"

For the first time, she doesn't blush. Instead, a wicked smile spreads across her face. She grabs her phone and turns on *Animal Magnetism* by Scorpions. She grinds her hips as her clothes come off, and I can't control myself. I unzip my jeans and stroke my dick, as I watch her. She licks her lips as she watches me.

"See something you like, sweetheart?" I ask.

"Watching you get yourself off is so fucking hot," she says in a smoky voice.

She stands before me, fully naked, and I cannot take my eyes off this goddess. After removing my clothes, I lay down on the bed.

"Baby, I want you to sit on my face. I'm craving your sweet pussy."

She climbs on top of me, giving me a close up view of her perfect little ass.

"Good girl. Now, get that hot little mouth around my dick."

She takes my entire length in her mouth as I tease her with my tongue. She moans and the vibrations drive me wild. I suck on her clit and her moans get louder. She's so fucking hot, I may never let her get dressed again. Running my hands along her sides, she giggles, sending more sensations up and down my dick. I feel her body quake as she comes undone, lips still firmly sliding up and down my cock until I lose control and fill her pretty mouth.

"Now, baby, I want to see you swallow me."

She swallows me and licks her lips, and I'm hard again.

"That's the first time I've ever done that," she whispers.

"Well, you were damn good at it."

"It felt amazing."

"That's my good girl. Now, I want your pussy wrapped around my dick. You're in for a long night, sweetheart."

"Good!"

Mel climbs on top of me as I impale her with my dick. Fuck. I can't get enough of being inside this goddess. She sits up straight and moves like she's belly dancing. I've felt nothing like it. I grab her hips as she rocks on top of me. I pull her tight against me and thrust in and out of her, loving how her skin feels against mine.

"Fuck, you're perfect."

She pulls herself back up. "I'm in charge this time," she says.

I growl as she leans back and rides me hard and fast. "So fuckin' good, sweetheart. Ride me harder, baby."

"Oh, Judd, so good. I love how you feel inside me."

Watching her sexy tits bouncing as she fucks me is too much to handle, and I fill her pussy.

"Fuck, I love when you come inside me," she screams as her body quakes. Her body bucks hard as she screams louder. She collapses against me and I hold her tight. I get hard again, and roll her over, my dick still inside her. Keeping my arms around her, we fuck again. Her nails rake over my back as I feel her body convulse with another powerful orgasm. I give her one last shot of cum before I collapse next to her and pull her tight against me. We kiss good night, and I hear Mel drift off to sleep.

"I love you," I whisper.

CHAPTER 6
Mel

What did he just say? My chest tightens and I can barely catch my breath. After making sure Judd's asleep, I slink out of bed and grab my clothes. I grab my phone and order a ride-share, then get dressed and wait for my ride. After I'm home, I get in bed and stare at the ceiling. What the hell did I just do? Tears stream down my face as I bury my head in my pillow.

I spend most of the day hiding in bed, finally getting up around dinner-time. A peanut butter and jelly sandwich is as much as I can stomach, and I only end up eating half. I realize how badly I screwed up, and it consumes me. I walk around like a zombie until I finally go to bed. I'm both relieved and sad that Judd didn't call, but I can't blame him after what I did.

When my alarm rings on Monday morning, I fight the temptation to throw it out the window. Instead, I drag my sorry ass out of bed and go through the motions of getting ready for work. I'm sitting in my office, staring at a blank monitor, when Jason pops his head in. He takes one look at me and comes in, sitting down across from me.

I'm lucky to have him. We came into the company together, both of us starting as interns. We quickly became friends, both of us having rotten luck in our love lives, but also having a lot of the same interests.

As handsome and well-built as he is, though, I never had any romantic feelings for him. He was more like the brother I never had.

"What's wrong? And don't you dare tell me nothing."

I drop my head onto the desk with a thud. "I fucked things up royally."

"With the cowboy?"

"Yeah."

"Talk to me, girl."

"We had an amazing night together on Saturday night. Just as we were falling asleep, I heard him whisper he loved me."

"Holy shit! That's huge. What did you say?"

"Nothing. I just left."

"You did WHAT?"

"I waited until he fell asleep and I called for a ride."

"Okay, you know I love you, right?"

"Yeah."

"Then you'll forgive me for saying this, but what the hell were you thinking?"

"I don't know."

"Come on, there's got to be a reason."

"Fine, but please, not in my office."

"Okay, how about drinks after work?"

"Sounds like exactly what I need."

"For now, how about coffee and something sinfully sweet?"

"I hear a cheese danish calling my name."

After drowning my sorrows in not one, but two danish, I faked my way through the workday then hit the company gym to work off the extra calories before heading home. The quiet loneliness was driving me nuts, so I headed out early to meet Jason at The Full Moon.

After finding an empty table, I sent Jason a text, and when a waitress named Tammy stopped by, I ordered myself a glass of Moscato. Tammy remembered me and asked if I would sing tonight. I wasn't sure I was up for it, but she begged, so I said I would.

"Hey, girl, glad you came," Jason said.

"I told you I would."

"Yeah, just wasn't sure you'd be up for it."

"I actually came early. My house is too quiet."

"You mean, without a certain cowboy making you scream?"

Lowering my head, I reply, "Yeah."

"Can I bring you a drink?" Tammy asked Jason.

"Corona in a bottle, please," Jason replied.

"Karaoke starts in a few," Tammy said to me before heading off to get Jason's beer.

"Karaoke?" Jason asked.

"She remembered me from the time I was here with Judd and asked me to sing tonight," I say.

"The time I saw the video of?"

"Yeah."

"Sure you're up for it?"

"No. But Tammy was so sweet that I said I would."

"I'll be here cheering you on, girl. But first, you still owe me an explanation from earlier."

"I'm too damaged for anyone to love."

"Why? Because Derek said you were?"

"Ouch. He's right, and he's not alone."

"What do you mean?"

"I tried dating after we split. And as soon as the discussion turned to future plans, that ended any chance at a relationship."

"Sweetie."

"And it's not me being over-sensitive. I took the honest approach and whenever the subject got to kids, I told them I couldn't conceive. Some of them had the courtesy to at least finish the date, but there were just as many who walked out before dinner arrived."

Jason lays a hand on my arm. "I'm so sorry, honey."

"Thanks."

Tammy walks up on stage. "Hey, everyone. We have a treat tonight. One-half of our new favorite duo is here, and she agreed to sing for us tonight. Please help me welcome Mel to the stage."

The crowd cheers, none louder than Jason, reminding me again why I'm so lucky he's my friend. I find the song I want and punch the number into the machine. The easily recognizable piano opening of Bonnie Tyler's *Total Eclipse of the Heart* fills the room. I'm about halfway through the song when I scan the crowd, hoping to catch sight of my cowboy. Well, my former cowboy. I finish the song and walk back to the table.

"Damn, girl, you sound even better live," Jason says.

"Thank you," I say as my cheeks heat.

"Time for our next singer," I hear Tammy say.

For the second time tonight, I hear a familiar piano opening. Steelheart's *Wait* is not that well-known a song, so I'm surprised to hear it. It's a sad but beautiful song, and my eyes mist up. But when I hear the voice that's singing it, the tears spill over. Turning to face the stage, I lock eyes with Judd. His hand is over his heart, his body hunches over, his eyes dark as he belts out the gut-wrenching lyrics, but it's the look on his face that stabs my heart. I caused that by running out on him and I hate myself for it. He races off the stage when he finishes the song.

"I need to get outta here," I say.

"Okay," Jason says. He grabs my arm and leads me out. We're just about to reach the door when Judd blocks our way.

"We need to talk," Judd says.

"I can't. I'm sorry," I reply.

"Please, Mel, please. I can't stand not being with you," Judd begs.

"You trust me, right?" Jason says.

"Yeah, of course," I say.

"Then please, you need to talk to him," Jason says.

"Okay," I say. "Where?"

"Our diner?" Judd asks.

I nod, then turn to Jason. "Thank you. I'll see you in the morning."

"Or you could take the day off. I'll tell them you're not feeling well and spending the day in bed," Jason says with a wink.

"That gets my vote," Judd says.

"Um, what's with ganging up on me?" I ask.

"I'll see you Wednesday morning," Jason says and heads to his car.

Judd and I stand in the parking lot for a minute before he says, "You still wanna go talk?"

"Yeah, but at my house. And you may want to stop home and pack a bag."

"You sure?"

"Yeah," I say.

"I'll see you soon."

Judd waits until I'm in my car before he gets in his truck. Butterflies fill my stomach when I hear his truck pull into my driveway. I know I need to tell him what I told Jason this morning, but I'm scared that he'll agree. Better to know now, I guess. I open the door and the butterflies go crazy.

"Please come in," I whisper.

"Thank you," Judd says. He walks in and lays an overnight bag by the door.

I lead him to the couch and we both sit. Turning to face him, I say, "I'm so sorry."

"No need to apologize."

"Yeah, there is. I shouldn't have left like that."

"Can I ask what happened?"

"The last man to say he loved me was Derek. And you know how that turned out."

"I'm not Derek."

"I know. You couldn't be further away from him. But that's not all it was."

"Tell me. I love you and I want to understand."

"I tried dating after the divorce was final. And every one of those dates failed. As soon as the topic got to family, and I told them about my problem, that was that. Some of them were kind enough to at least finish the date, but some actually left in the middle."

"Just because you couldn't have kids?"

"Yeah. After a few times, I finally gave up. Lexi and I thought we were destined to be single for the rest of our lives. Then she met Damien."

"That must have been hard for you."

"I was a bit jealous, but also happy for her. She deserved to find someone. So, I decided to try again and my first, and only, date I went on was a disaster. So, I gave up for a second time, feeling like everything Derek said was true. Feeling like no man would ever think I was enough. I just completely wrote off being with someone. Until..."

"What?"

"The sexiest man I ever laid eyes on kissed my hand. I tried like hell to fight what I felt for you, but you made it impossible. And then that damn shooting star."

"The night before the Halloween party?"

"Yeah. I made a wish that night. I wished that we would be together."

"I was sitting out back that night and saw it. I made the same wish."

"But, why?"

"Because the moment I laid eyes on you, I wanted you. And as much as that excited me, it also scared the hell out of me."

"I know exactly what you mean. What changed for you?"

"The more I got to know you, the more I trusted you. And trust isn't something I give easily."

"That means more to me than you know. I trust you too. And that's why I need to say one more thing."

"What?"

"I love you, Judd."

"I love you, Melissa."

He pulls me onto his lap and holds me tight. He claims my mouth, his tongue making his intentions quite clear, and I moan into his mouth. He puts his arm under my legs, stands, and carries me to my bedroom. He sets me down and says, "Baby, I hope you're well-rested."

"Is that so?"

"Oh yeah. I fully intend to spend the entire night making love to you."

"Mmm, Judd. Please, I want you so much."

"Do you remember the band Britny Fox?"

"Oh yeah. Dean Davidson is my favorite singer."

"Then you've heard his solo album?"

"I love Drive My Karma."

Judd smiles and grabs his phone. I hear the familiar opening notes of *Soul Soul*. Judd wraps his arms around me and holds me close while I circle his neck with my arms. As we dance, he sings the beautiful lyrics to me, and I melt, and at that moment, I surrender to his love.

"Please, Judd, take me to bed and make love to me."

In silence, he stands behind me, sliding his hands under my shirt.

His fingertips caress my skin as he removes my shirt and tosses it aside. He moves my hair aside and sucks on the back of my neck. The scent of his cologne fills my nose. The combination of cedar and citrus is intoxicating.

"Mine. All mine," he whispers in my ear, sending chills through my body. "Right?"

"Mmmm, I'm all yours."

"Good girl." My bra hits the floor, and I feel Judd's hands rub over my back. He comes around to my front and runs his tongue down the front of my throat, then between my breasts. Kneeling in front of me, he covers my stomach with kisses as he opens my jeans and slides them down. I step out of them and kick them aside.

Gazing at my hot pink thong, he says, "That's not the pink I want to see." Hooking his thumbs under the sides, he slides my panties off. "The most beautiful goddess I've ever seen," he says, still on his knees. I grab his shoulders to keep from going down. This man weakens me like nobody before him. He stands and I grab his shirt, tugging it off. I gawk at his sexy pecs while running my hands down his six-pack.

What I really want, however, is in his pants. I open his belt and his jeans. Sliding my hands over his firm ass, I slide his jeans down. His erection threatens to rip through his briefs and my mouth waters. I slide my hands inside the waistband and free the beast, unable to take my eyes off of his naked body.

"Somethin' you like, darlin'?" he asks.

"Oh, hell yeah! And I want it now."

"My, my. So eager, my love."

He carries me over to the bed and lays me down. He joins me and covers my body with his. I feel his tongue sweeping my mouth as he crushes his lips to mine. After a toe-curling kiss, he wastes no time. He moves his head between my legs and holy shit! His tongue swipes up and down my pussy at a feverish pace. Words no longer exist and all I can do is moan at the way he makes me feel. I give my sexy cowboy a smack on his ass.

"Naughty, woman," he says before his mouth returns to my pussy. He sucks on me and finishes me off. I scream at the top of my lungs as my body bounces. "You taste so good, my sweet Melissa. What do you want now, my love?"

"I want your cock as deep inside me as you can."

"Wait right there."

"Couldn't move if I tried."

I watch Judd grab a couple of throw pillows from the chair. "Lift up that cute little ass." I raise my hips and he slides the pillows under me. "Comfortable, baby?" he asks.

"Mmm, yeah."

He blankets me with his perfectly chiseled body and slowly slides the entire length of his dick inside me. "So good, sweetheart. Fucking heaven."

Wrapping my arms around him, I pull him close as he moves inside me. Something's different this time. So much more than mind-blowing sex. Our eyes lock, and remain that way the entire time. His pace suddenly quickens and I know he's close. He growls as he empties himself inside me. After moving onto his back, he pulls me in tight and I lay my head on his sweaty chest. Inhaling his musk invigorates my senses and I whisper a moan.

"Oh, Judd, I finally know what it feels like to make love."

"You noticed too? It felt different. Even more incredible."

Tears fill my eyes as I gaze up at my man. "I love you, Judd."

"I love you, Melissa."

CHAPTER 7
Judd

The winter sun streams in through Mel's bedroom window, waking me. I look over at my beautiful goddess, still sound asleep. The sound of her soft snores warms my heart. I slip out of bed, pull on a pair of gray sweatpants and tiptoe to Mel's kitchen. After putting on a pot of coffee, I gather the ingredients to make French toast.

"Good morning, my sexy cowboy," Mel says.

She's wearing a pink fuzzy over-sized robe. Her hair is a matted mess after last night's passion and damn, she's the cutest woman I've ever laid eyes on.

"Good morning, my love."

I look over and notice her eyes firmly planted on my crotch. Clearing my throat, I say, "Excuse me. My eyes are up here." She laughs and my dick stirs. After finishing breakfast, we get naked and get back in bed. We're lying on our sides facing each other, talking.

"Can I ask you something, and it's okay if you don't wanna answer?" I ask.

"Can I hear the question first?"

"Sure. Why don't you want Lexi and Damien to know about us?"

"It's not that I have a problem with them, but I know how Lexi is."

"Meaning?"

"She's super-romantic and loves relationships, but she can be a bit over-zealous."

"I'm still a little confused."

"The first time I saw, I said you were attractive, and she's been bugging me ever since. Not in a bad way, just constantly. I just want some time to enjoy us first."

"And have you been? Enjoying us?"

"Oh, yeah. And trust me, it's more than just the sex. Not that the sex hasn't been incredible, but I love the way you make me feel. Like I'm actually worth something."

"Sweetheart, you're worth everything. I love you."

"I love you so much."

"Now, get yourself bundled up. I have something fun planned for us."

We drive to our town's high school and park. I walk to the bed of the truck and grab two sleds. When Mel sees them, she squeals.

"I haven't been sledding since I was a kid."

"I've never done it."

"Oooh, we're gonna have fun."

I put the sleds down at the top of the hill and we both sit.

"What do I do?" I ask.

"Watch me."

Mel uses her cute little bottom to slide the sled back and forth. When she gets a path started, she pushes off and flies down the hill. I can hear her giggling all the way up here. Suddenly feeling nervous, I just sit there.

"What'cha waiting for?" she yells.

"Not so sure about this now."

"You can do it, my big bad sexy cowboy."

She takes her hands and makes antlers on the side of her, sticking her tongue out as she waves her hands. She's in trouble now! I take off and when I'm at the bottom, I grab her and pull her down in the snow.

"Hey!"

"Your fault for teasing me."

"So, you wanna go again?"

"Yeah, let's go."

We grab our sleds and race up the hill. After a few more times up and down the hill, I pull her down in the snow again.

"I wasn't teasing this time."

"I know." I lay on my back and start making a snow angel. Mel lays next to me and makes her own angel. When we're done, we lay there holding hands, gazing at each other. Moments like these are some of my favorites with her. Of course, being naked with her is my top favorite, but these are a close second. I see her shivering, so I stand and help her up.

"How 'bout we go get in our jammies and relax in front of the fireplace until dinner," I say.

"That sounds perfect."

We're sitting, huddled under a blanket, sipping cocoa. Mel puts her head on my shoulder and says, "Thanks for today. It was so much fun."

"My pleasure. I had a blast, but now I'm starving."

"I was planning on making meatloaf tonight, if you like that," Mel says.

"Very much. What do you usually make with it?"

"Mashed potatoes and creamed spinach."

"Mmm, you really know how to please a man, sweetheart."

"In the kitchen and the bedroom," she says with a wink and now all I can think about is getting her back in bed.

"Well, put me to work, baby."

"Would you mind peeling potatoes?"

"Not at all."

Mel hands me the bag of potatoes and I get to work. She grabs the meat and gets that mixed and formed. Watching her hands work that meat is driving me wild. Wait until I get her on that counter later! We finish getting the rest of the food prepared and have an hour to kill until dinner is ready. I turn some music on and take her hand. "Come dance with me, my love." I pull her close and we sway together. I get so lost in her, the kitchen timer startles me.

"Back to work, cowboy," she teases. She gets the potatoes mashed, and the spinach finished at exactly the same time as the meatloaf is done. I grab that from the oven and slice it.

"Mmm, looks and smells delicious, Mel. Oh, and the food looks good too." She giggles and I swear there is no better sound.

As we're cleaning up after dinner, she asks, "What do you wanna do tonight?"

"I actually brought something I thought you would enjoy."

"Hmmm, I like the sound of that."

"Down, woman," I tease. "Come with me to the couch."

I sit and pat the cushion next to me. She curls up and leans into me. I grab a book out of my overnight bag. "Since you fell asleep last time, I thought we could try again."

"Ooh, sounds perfect."

I cover Mel with a blanket and pull her in tight, then open the book. She rests her head against my chest as I read to her. I think this might be the most perfect moment I've ever experienced. After a few hours, she yawns.

"I'm sorry. That wasn't because of you reading," Mel says.

"I know, baby. Let's get you to bed."

"Will you stay again?"

"I'd love nothing more."

I pick her up and carry her to her bedroom. She's asleep as soon as her pretty head hits the pillow. I spoon her and fall asleep to the rhythmic sound of her breathing. Work and helping Lexi with her wedding plans keep her occupied for the rest of the week and not being with her is killing me. We talk every night, but it's not the same as holding her. I check out The Full Moon and see they are having a country night tonight, so I give Mel a quick call at her normal lunchtime.

"Hey, cowboy," she says when she answers.

"Hey, beautiful. The Moon's having country karaoke night. Up for it?"

"I'd love to."

"Great. I've missed you this week. Oh, and it's also a costume party for anyone who wants."

"I have just the outfit."

"Mmm, I can't wait to see it. I'll pick you up at five and we can grab dinner there, if you'd like. And make sure you pack an overnight bag."

"Can't wait."

"Me either. I love you."

"I love you more."

I disconnect and get back to the stables to finish my work. But all I can focus on is my angel, and I can't wait to see her tonight. When I get to her house and knock, my jaw drops when she opens the door.

"Holy shit, baby."

"Something you like."

"Damn right."

"Well, I'm a bit disappointed. I expected to see you in assless chaps."

"Oh my god, Mel!"

She gives me that giggle I love so much, and as if her denim shorts, cowgirl boots and her red blouse tied at the waist aren't enough, that giggle puts me over the edge. She grabs her long winter coat and we head out. The party is already in full swing when we arrive. We find an empty table, put our coats down and hit the dance floor. Brett Eldredge's *Mean to Me* is playing, and I pull her in close.

She pulls my head down and whispers in my ear. "I forgot something."

"What?"

"My panties."

My jaw drops and all I can think about is getting inside those sexy little shorts. We take a seat when the song ends.

"Hey, you two lovebirds," Tammy says when she approaches our table. "Somethin' to drink?"

"Moscato for me," Mel says.

"Coors in the bottle for me," I say.

"Here's a menu. Be right back with the drinks."

"Thanks," Mel says.

"What're you thinkin' for dinner?" I ask.

"A burger. I want to bite into a big juicy pile of meat."

Damn, this woman! She's left me unable to speak. I watch a wicked grin spread across her gorgeous face.

"What?" I say.

"Cat got your tongue?" she says with a wink.

"It will later."

"I sure hope so, sexy!"

We're just finishing dinner when Tammy heads up to the stage.

"Hey ya'll! It's country night and we have a special treat to kick things off. Put your hands together for our favorite couple, Mel and Judd."

I grab Mel's hand and we join Tammy. She hands Mel the microphone first. Shania Twain's *Any Man of Mine* starts. I can't take my eyes off my sexy cowgirl as she dances while belting out the tune. She's met with a huge round of applause when she finishes, then hands the mic to me. I choose *Country Girl* by Luke Bryan. Mel dances along while I sing and it's a miracle my dick didn't rip a hole in my jeans.

I rush her off the stage and right to the men's room.

"What are we doing in here?" she says.

"Get your hot little ass up on that counter," I say.

She jumps up on the counter and opens her legs for me. I open her shorts and slide my hand inside.

"Fuck, baby."

"Oh, yeah, that's my other surprise."

I tug at her shorts and she lifts her ass for me. After her shorts are on the floor, I spread her legs wide and gaze at her freshly groomed pussy. I get on my knees and bury my tongue inside her. I lick her hard and fast, and she quickly explodes on my face.

"On your feet. Now turn and face the mirror. You're going to watch yourself take me, baby."

She stands in front of me and I rub her sweet little ass before I drop my jeans and briefs around my ankles.

"Hold on tight, woman."

She grabs the counter and lowers her head.

"No! I said you're going to watch."

"But, I'm not pr-"

"Don't even think about finishing that sentence. You're the most beautiful woman I've ever known. Now lift that head up and watch us fuck."

She locks eyes with me in the mirror as I grab my dick and slide inside her pussy. She's still slick from her orgasm, and I slide in and out of her with ease. I come inside her hard and fast, then we quickly get dressed and return to our table. We're about to get up and hit the dance floor when I see Mel's face fall.

"Guess they'll let just anyone in," Mel's sister Trish spits.

"Please, just go away and leave me alone," Mel says.

Trish turns to me and says, "How much she payin' you?"

"I beg your pardon," I say.

"To sit here with her," Trish says.

"What makes you think she needs to pay someone?" I ask.

"Oh, she hasn't told you she's useless and damaged. Not to mention how she treated our dad," Trish says.

My blood boils. I take a deep breath and stand. "Your sister is the kindest, sweetest, sexiest, most beautiful woman I've ever met and damn, does she know how to pleasure my dick. So, go back to your table and wallow in your pathetic misery while I take this incredible woman home and make love to her until the sun comes up."

Mel stands and I help her into her coat. I put my arm around her and we head out to the parking lot. We get in my truck and her eyes spill over.

"I'll understand if you wanna take me home," she says.

"Why would you think that?"

"I'm too much drama."

"The hell you are. That drama was your sister's fault, not yours."

"But what she said is-"

"What she said is the biggest load of bullshit I've ever heard. You're none of the things she said and all the things I did."

"But-"

"Stop-"

I drive us to the park and turn to her. "Listen to me please, sweetheart. I'm in love with you. I've meant everything I said. You're beautiful, sexy, intelligent, and kind. Exactly the type of woman I always wanted to find. And damn, baby, you're hotter than hell in bed, or wherever we fuck. You don't think I'm a liar, do you?"

"Of course not."

"Then you need to believe me."

"I want to."

"Then do it. Look, I know the negative is easier to believe. I've been there. Sometimes I still am. What keeps me going is your love."

"How did I get so lucky?"

"I ask myself that every time you're in my arms."

"I'm in love with you, too."

"So, then you'll still come home with me tonight?"

"But I have work tomorrow."

"I'll drive you."

We're lying in bed, holding each other. "Can I ask you about something Trish said?"

"About my dad?"

"Yeah. Only if you want."

"I told you about him getting hooked on drugs. Well, he had also smoked most of his life and developed COPD. It eventually took him."

"I'm so sorry."

"Thanks. I wish that was it and I promise, I'll tell you everything. After dealing with everything alone, I'm just not yet in a place to talk about it."

"Sweetheart, that's so much more than anyone should have to take."

"Yet, I have. I just can't talk about anything else tonight. I hope you understand."

"Of course. I know I understand. I know it can't be easy to talk about."

"It's not, but I know I need to. And I know you won't judge me."

"I'm glad. Please know that I'll always be on your side."

She gently puts her hand on my face. "I know. I'll never be able to thank you enough."

"You already have."

CHAPTER 8

Mel

"O'Laughlin Consulting. Melissa McNeill."

"Oh shit, I hit the wrong button. Meant to call your cell."

"No worries, what's up?"

"Called to make sure you were ready for tonight?" Lexi asks.

"Why wouldn't I be?"

"No reason, just checking. Sure you're okay?"

"Yeah."

"See you tonight."

"Later."

How the hell am I going to get through tonight, pretending not to be with Judd? I hope Lexi will be so wrapped in Damien that she'll forget I'm there. Part of me wants to tell her, but I just can't. Especially now, this close to the wedding. A sudden feeling of darkness fills my office and when I look up, I see Daniel standing in my doorway.

"Good morning, Daniel. Can I help you?"

"That's Mr. O'Laughlin to you."

"I beg your pardon?"

"You will address me properly."

"You're not my superior and this is the twenty-first century."

"Oh, honey, I'm superior to you in every way."

70

"I'm not your honey."

"You could be."

I take a deep breath as my blood boils. "No, I couldn't. Now, is there something I can do for you?"

"Nope."

"Enjoy the rest of your day, Daniel."

I sit at my desk and fume for a few minutes before diving into my work. Jason drops by around noon so we can grab lunch.

"You look pissed," Jason says.

I tell him about my encounter with 'Little Richard.'

"Good thing I didn't hear that, or I'd be looking for a new job. Are you going to report him?"

"Not this time, but I did document the encounter."

"Good. So, on a happier topic, what're you and the cowboy up to tonight?"

"Pretending."

"Huh?"

"Group outing with Lexi and Damien."

"And they still don't know?"

"Not yet."

"Why not?"

"Fear."

"I don't understand. What are you afraid of?"

"Jinxing it."

"Come on, Mel. That's ridiculous."

"Because I've had so much luck in the past."

"I get it, but I think you're making a mistake."

"Maybe, but it's what I need to do."

"Well, have fun anyway."

"We always do."

"Hey, favor when we get back from lunch."

"What?"

"Pretend something is wrong with your computer so I can hang out and pretend to fix it."

"You got it! Watch this," I say when I see Little Richard. "Don't forget, I need you to check my computer."

Daniel glances over as Jason says, "Does now work?"

"Yes, thank you."

When we get to my office, I whisper, "Wanna place a bet on how long it takes for him to appear?"

Sure enough, about fifteen minutes later, Daniel appears. I give Jason's foot a tap with mine. He looks at the doorway then says, "See this here? There are two versions of this application. I've had a few others report this after the last release."

"What do I need to do?" I ask.

"Nothing. I need to remove both versions then push the latest update to your machine. This will take a while, so let me get started."

"Thank you. Mr. O'Laughlin, is there something you need?" I ask.

He shakes his head no and walks away. I hold back on commenting in case he's listening outside the door. Jason clicks the mouse and some keys to make it sound like he's fixing my computer. I look at my screen and see a Word document open with about ten different euphemisms for a certain male body part. I try to remain professional, but my Beavis and Butt-head maturity level wins and I double over, barely able to breathe.

"You need to get that off my screen before anyone sees," I beg.

"No worries, the IT dude has ya covered."

A little before four, my assistant Allie appears in the doorway. "You have a visitor," she says, her face flushed. I don't need to ask who it is.

"Ready to go, love?" Judd asks.

"You bet," I say. "Allie, feel free to head out early today. Paid, of course."

"Thank you," Allie says and heads back to her desk.

I barely survive the group karaoke outing. What was I thinking, singing *Eternal Flame*. And then telling Lexi I'm falling for Judd. Why can't I just keep my trap shut? I manage to convince her nothing is going on between us, but with the wedding plans, it's getting harder and harder not to tell her the truth. I'm especially nervous I won't be able to hide our relationship since we're walking together at the wedding. Turning my focus to Lexi helps keep me distracted. When it comes my turn to walk down the aisle, I can't take my eyes off of Judd. He looks so damn good in his tuxedo that I want to rip it off of him.

After the ceremony, we're walking out, arms linked, and I can barely contain myself.

"You're stunning," he whispers in my ear, and I shiver.

"Thanks, handsome."

The nice thing about being the best man and maid of honor is everyone expecting us to dance together, so we don't get too many questions. Between New Year's and the Super Bowl, Judd and I have had to spend time in group settings. It's getting tougher to keep our secret, and I think Lexi might already know. But we soldier on. When Damien plans a group outing to attend the Super Bowl parade after our Eagles win, I claim to have to work and skip it. We're only a couple of days away from Valentine's Day, and at least I know there won't be a group outing for that one. I'm knee deep in tax preparation when Lexi calls.

"Hey, the guys are having a poker night tonight, so the wives are going out. Would you like to join us?"

"Thanks, but I have a lot of work to do, so I'll be here late tonight."

"Okay. Talk to you soon."

"Bye, Lexi."

"Okay, what's with the fibbing?" Jason says after I disconnect.

"Truth?"

"Yeah. Talk to me."

"Lexi fits in with the other rocker wives. I don't."

"I don't believe that. You're the coolest chick ever!"

"Thanks. But honestly, not me putting myself down. It's just not what I'm into. They like to party as much as possible, but I prefer quiet nights at home. It's one of many ways Judd is so perfect for me."

"So, any plans yet for Valentine's Day?"

"Judd hasn't said anything. Maybe he's tired of me."

"Okay, crazy. I've seen the way that dude looks at you. Trust me, he's not tired of you. He looks like he wants to eat you."

"Oooh, and he's good at that."

"Melissa!"

"Oh, please, don't act all innocent, Jason."

We're laughing so hard, we don't hear Daniel stop by. He walks over to my desk and slams his hand down so hard that my pencil cup spills.

"What the hell is going on in here?" Daniel shouts.

"We were just letting off a little steam," Jason says.

"Well, do that shit on your own time." Daniel turns to me. "And you are skating on thin ice. You're lucky my uncle thinks so highly of you. But you better watch your back. I have a lot of college buddies that would kill for your job. And for a lot less money."

I sit at my desk, too shell-shocked to speak. Jason and I just stare at each other. We look up when we hear movement and Allie walks over.

"I'm so sorry. That was my fault," Allie says.

"It absolutely was not," I say.

"I had to run to the copier, so I wasn't at my desk to warn you."

"Not at all your fault or your job to warn me. I can handle what that little jerk dishes out," I say.

"Okay," Allie says and turns to head back to her desk.

"One thing, though," I say. "If he ever speaks to you that way, please let me know."

"I will. Thank you."

"Why does it feel like he has it out for me?" I ask Jason.

"I don't know, but I agree."

"He's damn lucky Judd didn't hear that."

"That's for sure."

We finish up and head out to the parking lot. I'm not looking forward to a night alone, but I just don't feel comfortable around the other girls. I decide to take advantage of Judd having a guy's night. I pour myself a glass of wine, draw a bubble bath, and grab the contemporary romance novel I picked up. The smuttier, the better for me, especially if I get new ideas to try with the cowboy.

I feel more relaxed after my bath. I put on my favorite jammies and make myself a grilled cheese sandwich for dinner. I rarely put the TV on, but tonight, I need some comfort viewing, so I go with my favorite eighties movies, Sixteen Candles, Pretty in Pink, and The Breakfast Club. I'm just about at the end of The Breakfast Club when I hear a familiar vehicle pull into my driveway. What's Judd doing here?

I open the door and my heart drops when I see the look on his face.

"Come in. What's going on?" I say. "I thought it was guys' night.

Judd sits down on the couch. His forehead is wrinkled, his eyes lowered. He sighs, his mouth in a slight frown. "Am I enough for you?"

"What do you mean?"

"I'm not as extravagant as the other guys, and I don't have all the free time in the world like they do."

"And?"

"Wouldn't you rather have the life the other girls do?"

"Do you know why I'm home right now?"

"Because you had to work late."

"No. That's what I told Lexi. The truth is, I'm not like those girls and I'm uncomfortable around them."

"Really?"

"Yeah. Tell me, what brought this on?"

"The other guys were talking about their Valentine's Day plans and I was afraid you would be let down when I told you my plan."

"Are we going to be together?"

"Of course!"

"Then I'm going to love it."

"But you haven't heard it."

"Doesn't matter. I just wanna be with you. But I am excited to hear."

"I'm going to cook you dinner and make you a special dessert, followed by a luxurious soak in the tub, and, well, anything else you want."

"That sounds great, but I would like to slightly change the plan."

"How so?"

"Valentine's Day shouldn't be just about me, but about us. So, I want to do all of it together."

"Baby, you're unlike any woman I've ever known. Just one other thing. What would you like?"

"For dinner?"

"No, for a gift."

"Nothing. Something else you need to know about me is I don't believe in that."

"But men are supposed to buy their women gifts."

"Says who? You've already given me the greatest gift in the world. Your love."

"I love you, sweetheart. Thanks for making me feel better."

"My pleasure."

"It will be on Valentine's Day. I'll come pick you up after Damien drops the dogs off."

"I can't wait. And I would love to take care of the grocery shopping. What did you have in mind for dinner?"

"You like seafood?"

"Definitely."

"How about flounder stuffed with crabmeat?"

"That sounds delicious."

"I can't wait."

"Me either."

Judd plants a kiss on my lips that leaves me desperate for more. I have a feeling Valentine's Day is going to be incredible. The next couple of days at work drag. I do my best to avoid Daniel after the other day. The one time I happened to pass him, I was met with a sneer, but nothing more. I get back to my office and see a beautiful bouquet of roses on Allie's desk.

"They're beautiful," I say.

"My new boyfriend sent them."

"So sweet. What are your plans for Valentine's Day?"

"He said it's a surprise."

"Tell you what. Why don't you take the rest of the day off? Paid."

"Are you sure?"

"Absolutely. Go pamper yourself and get ready for your date!"

"Thank you, Melissa."

"You're welcome."

Jason stops by my office on his way out. "Hey, girl. When you getting outta here?"

"Soon. Damien and Lexi already left, so Judd's picking me up when I get home."

"Guess you won't need to bring any clothes."

"Hey, I won't be naked the whole time."

We both laugh quietly, just in case the little dickhead is nearby. I grab a quick shower and pack myself a bag, including some brand new lingerie. My body tingles from head to toe at the mere thought of spending the weekend with my sexy man. I can only imagine what he has in store for me. When Judd arrives, he helps me carry everything to his truck and we head back to his ranch.

"You look even more beautiful than you usually do, my love."

"You're so sweet, my handsome cowboy."

We get back to the ranch and the first thing I notice is a pair of red tapers and a bouquet of daisies on Judd's dining room table.

"I know you said no gifts, but I had to get something, so those are for both of us," Judd says.

I throw my arms around him and claim his mouth like he's done to me so many times. He picks me up and I wrap my legs around him while he firmly plants his powerful hands on my ass.

"I want you so much," I whisper.

"I want you too, but you must wait, my love. I have a surprise for you later."

"Mmm. I like the sound of that. Let's get dinner going."

Once the food's ready, Judd dims the lights and lights both tapers. He pours two glasses of wine while I plate the food. After everything's on the table, Judd walks to my chair and pulls it out for me. Such a gentleman! Judd lifts his glass. "To us and the love we've found together," he says.

"To us," I say, and we clink glasses. After we finish eating and cleaning up, we head to the living room and play with Maggie and Dave for a while, until they're tuckered out and curl up on their beds.

"Wait here. I have a surprise for you, baby," Judd says and hurries off to his bedroom.

"I need to freshen up, so I'll be in the bathroom," I say. Grabbing my bag, I shut the door behind me and change into the red satin nightie I bought. I decide to skip the panties, so my cowboy has easier access to the place I most want him to touch. I return to the couch, pull my hair into a ponytail, and wait for him.

"Are you ready for your surprise, my love?"

"Oh, yeah, babe."

Judd walks out of the bedroom and my jaw hits the floor. He stands in front of me wearing nothing but a pair of black leather chaps, buckled at the waist. His dick was hidden in a pouch in front and he topped the outfit with a black suede cowboy hat. He walks over to the stereo, giving me a delightful view of his hot, naked ass. I hear Big and Rich's Save a Horse Ride a Cowboy start. Judd stands in front of me and grinds his hips.

"Yee-haw, sexy cowboy," I shout.

Judd turns around and his hot ass is right in front of me. I can't control my hands and I give him a smack on each cheek. His muscles drive me wild and I can't keep my hands off of him. By the time the song ends, I'm so turned on, my pussy throbs.

"Damn, that was so fuckin' sexy. But, now it's my turn," I say. "Have a seat."

CHAPTER 9

Judd

My sexy Melissa turns on Touch Me by Samantha Fox and treats me to a sexy dance of her own. I can't take my eyes off her gorgeous body as she shakes those sexy tits and ass for me. When she's done, she walks over and leans in, her hands on my thighs. Mel puts a pillow on the floor and kneels in front of me, running her hand over the pouch holding my dick.

"My very own feed bag," she says as she unbuckles my chaps. She pulls my already-hard dick out and takes the entire length in her mouth. She stops long enough to say, "I wanna suck your cock until you fill my mouth with your cum."

"Oh fuck, baby."

I groan as she returns her mouth to my dick, sucking me slow. Her tongue slides along my shaft. Fuck, those pouty lips feel so good on my dick. She runs her hands along my chest while she sucks me off. She moves her hands down and teases my balls. I growl as my balls tighten and my warm cream pours down her throat.

"Damn, woman, you're so fucking good at that. And now, I get to return the favor. Get your sexy little ass on the couch and spread those legs."

She sits down and opens her legs wide, showing her freshly shaved pussy.

"Good girl. Such a pretty little pussy glistening for me."

I kneel in front of her, worshiping my goddess. I lift her sexy ass off the couch and slide my tongue up and down her pussy. She thrusts into my mouth and her desperation turns me on even more.

"Baby, stand up on the couch and face the back. Now, spread those legs and hold on tight."

"Mmm, Judd."

I sit down between her legs.

"Nice view, sweetheart. You're so damn sexy. I wanna feel that hot little pussy sliding along my mouth."

She rocks her hips back and forth, moaning as her pussy glides along my tongue. I smack her sexy little ass. "You're such a naughty girl."

"I want more."

"More what?"

"That."

"That what? Tell me one of your dirty desires."

"I want you to put me over your knee and spank me."

"Damn, woman. But first, I want you to come on my face."

I slip my fingers inside her soaking wet pussy while I suck her clit hard. Her legs shake as her moans increase in volume. I stroke her g-spot hard until I feel her love rain down on me. She screams as her body bucks above me. I get up and grab a towel to clean my face. I help her down from the couch.

"You've been quite the naughty girl. I think you might need to be punished."

I smile as she lies on my lap. Damn, that sexy little ass, just begging for my hand. I give her a light smack and she moans.

"Harder, baby."

Fuck! I give her a harder smack and she moans again. "Mmm, so good, Judd."

After giving her a few more swats, her cheeks are pink. I stroke her bottom. "Are you okay, baby?"

"Oh yeah, so good. I've always wanted to do that."

"Any other desires you wanna share tonight?"

"Maybe, but I wanna hear one of yours first."

"I wanna record a video."

She says nothing and I'm afraid I crossed a line.

"Um, that sounds hot."

"You really wanna do it?"

"Yeah. I wanna see us fuck."

I scoop her up and throw her over my shoulder. Her satin nightie feels amazing against my skin, but I can't wait to rip it off of her. I put her down and grab my tripod and video camera out of the closet. "I've never used this with a woman. I usually only videotape wildlife. Tonight, that all changes."

After I turn the camera on, I look at Mel and my dick springs to life again. "Okay, baby, I want that nightie on the floor. Now!"

She lifts the nightie over her head and drops it on the floor. Fuck, she's a goddess. "On the bed, now, my love."

She climbs onto the bed and crawls across it, glancing over at the camera and fuck if it's not the sexiest thing I've ever seen. I thought she'd be shy, but the camera makes her even more wild.

"Okay, my sexy cowboy. Get your hot naked body up here. I need your cock inside me now!"

She runs her hands down her body, stopping to tease her pussy for the camera, and I almost blow my load right there.

"On your back. Now! I wanna ride that cock like it's never been ridden before."

Holy. Fucking. Shit. This woman!

She climbs on top of me and grabs my dick. Stroking it with the soft hands, she purrs, "Mmm, this hot hard dick is going to feel so good inside me." She lifts her body and lowers herself onto my dick, slowly taking every inch of me inside her soaking wet pussy. She sits up straight and licks her lips as she slides up and down my dick. I grab her ass and squeeze, and she rides me, her sexy breasts bouncing.

"Oh, fuck, my sweet Melissa, you're so fucking good."

"Mmm, Judd, you feel amazing inside me. Oh, god, oh Judd."

She increases her pace and her moans match as I feel her body quake. She drenches my dick as she orgasms, and it feels so damn good. Her gorgeous body bucks hard as the waves of pleasure consume her.

"I want you on all fours."

She climbs off and does as she's told, facing the camera. I get on my knees behind her, grab my cock, and with one quick motion, I'm as deep inside her as I can. I grab her ponytail and pull her head back.

"Mmm, Judd."

"You like that, baby?"

"Oh, fuck, yeah."

"Good girl. I want the camera to see your pretty face while I fuck you." I pound her sweet pussy hard. The sound of my flesh slapping hers is so fucking hot. "Rub your clit while I fuck you."

She moans as she rubs her clit and it sounds so damn sweet. I can't hold back any longer and I empty my cock inside her. I can't help but wonder just how wild she'll get for the camera.

"On your back and face the camera. Good girl. Now spread those legs wide."

I go to my dresser and grab a vibrator I bought just for tonight. Handing it to her, I flash her a wicked grin. I move the chair so I have a better view of her. She turns the vibrator all the way up and presses it against her clit. She arches her back as she gets herself off.

"That vibrator better not leave that sweet little pussy."

"Mmm, Judd."

She moans and looks over at me, licking her lips. Just that sexy little look and my dick's throbbing for her. I grab my hand and stroke.

"Get your ass over here and fuck my face."

Who is this woman? I race over to the bed, get on all fours, and hover over my wild woman. I position myself so my dick's over her head. She reaches up, grabs me, and guides me into her mouth. I take the vibrator from her and press it harder against her clit. She screams out as she comes over and over. Her screams send me over the edge and I come right down her throat. I get up and turn the camera off.

"I can barely move," Mel whispers, a wide smile filling her face. I pick her up and position her on her side of the bed, then lay next to her.

"Baby, that was the most incredible thing I've ever experienced. I was afraid you wouldn't like it or you'd be nervous, but damn, baby, you shocked the hell out of me."

"I need to confess something. I loved being on camera."

"So you like being watched?"

"Yeah, but to be clear, only by you. This," she says, pointing at her naked body, "is for your eyes only."

"Good. Because you're mine and I'm not willing to share."

"But, let me guess, I need to share you, if you want?"

"First, I don't want, and second, absolutely not."

"Someone shoulda told Derek that."

"Fuck that asshole. Anyone who throws someone like you away is an ass."

"I love you."

"I love you, sweetie."

We lay in silence until I hear Mel whisper, "I wanna watch the video."

"You sure?"

"Yeah. I mean, I think so. Do you?"

"Yeah."

I get up and plug the camera into my TV and grab the remote. After climbing back into bed, I pull Mel in tight and press play. I watch her face when she sees herself. Her face reddens a bit, and she giggles, but never looks away. She watches herself riding me and says, "We look damn good together."

"We sure as hell do, baby."

We finish watching and I turn the TV off. Mel grabs my hand and puts it between her legs.

"Holy shit, woman. You're soaked."

"The video got me all horny. I need you inside me. Please, baby," Mel begs.

Blanketing her with my body, I slide inside her. Damn, this woman feels like heaven. She throws her arms around me and pulls me against her.

"Please, Judd, I wanna make love this time."

"Mmm, my sweet Melissa."

Our bodies move together in the sensual dance of two people in love. Two people completely lost in each other. Two people becoming one, knocking down the walls we've been building and giving ourselves to each other. As incredible as our sex has been, it's different this time. I can't explain, but damn, it feels amazing. We climax together, both of us completely spent.

We're in the bathroom getting ready for bed. Mel stands with her legs closed tight, wiggling.

"What the hell?" I tease.

She points at the toilet, but doesn't say a word.

"It's okay to pee in front of me."

She turns red and shakes her head no.

"The same woman who just made a sex tape with me won't pee in front of me," I tease.

She shoots daggers at me and wiggles more. "I'm afraid I might fart," she whispers.

"And? You're human and humans fart," I say, laughing.

"I can't do that in front of you," she squeals.

"What if we started living together? You couldn't hold your farts."

"Oh my god, stop talking about farts," she says, then sits on the toilet and covers her lap with a towel.

Laughing, I walk out of the bathroom and wait outside the door. When she comes out, she gives me a light smack on the ass. "That's for picking on me," she teases and darts past me. I catch her, pick her up and toss her onto the bed, both of us in hysterics. This woman really has it all. Looks, brains, a sense of humor, and wild in bed. I'll never understand how anyone let her slip away. We snuggle under the covers, and she's out like a light. The sound of her soft snores lulls me to sleep.

I wake up alone the following morning to the most delicious smell. When I get to the kitchen, Mel's standing at the stove. I see two plates with silver dollar pancakes on them. The skillet is filled with strawberries, blueberries, raspberries, and blackberries.

"Mmm, baby, it smells amazing."

"Whole wheat pancakes with roasted berries. It's almost ready."

When she's done, Mel spoons berries over the pancakes and lightly dusts them with powdered sugar. While we eat, I ask her, "What would you like to do today?"

"I'd love to see the barn, especially your horses."

"You got it."

Mel bounces and claps her hands. "I can't wait."

She runs to the bedroom with me hot on her heels. We grab a quick shower and get dressed, then head out to the barn. Mel beelines to the stables and just stands there, a wide grin on her face. "I thought you only had two horses," she says. "And why does one door not have a name on it?"

"She's new. I just bought her a couple of days ago."

"She looks just like my childhood horse."

"I know."

"What's her name?"

"That's up to you."

"Why me?"

"She's yours."

"What? Are you kidding?" she squeals.

"I'm not kidding, darlin'. I could see the sparkle leave your eyes when you talked about Dolly. "Since she's yours, you get to pick her name."

Mel walks over to her and pets her new horse's head and gets nuzzled. "She likes you, sweetie."

"So, pretty girl, what's your name?"

I watch Mel whisper something in the horse's ear. She puts her head on Mel's shoulder and Mel looks over at me. "Her name is JoJo. Short for Joanna."

A warmth washes over me as I hear Mel name her horse after my mother. I pull her close and my voice cracks as I whisper, "Thank you, baby."

JoJo nuzzles us both and we know she approves of her name. Mel helps me feed all three horses. I take her around the rest of the barn and she helps with the other animals as well. She looks up at the loft and says, "Hmmm, we could have some fun up there."

"You're insatiable, baby. But, honestly, I had the same thought not long after we got together."

"Your fault for being too damn sexy!"

"I may need to do some decorating up there."

"Oh, yeah? What are you thinking?"

"Uh, maybe a bed."

"I think that would be perfect."

As we're walking out of the barn, I say, "Since it's warmer than normal today, how about we get Dave and Maggie and take a walk around the ranch?"

"I'd love to."

Taking her hand in mine, we walk the perimeter of the ranch until we end up at the weeping willow tree in the corner.

"Oh, wow. This bench is beautiful. Is that your mom?" Mel asks.

"Yes. When I first moved here, I saw someone selling handmade benches. I had her picture printed on a piece of wood and added to the bench."

"The intricacy of the butterfly is stunning, but not nearly as stunning as your mom."

"Thank you. That's her high school senior picture."

Mel gazes at Mom's pictures and tears fill her eyes. To see my girlfriend look at my mom like that warms my heart in a way I didn't know was possible. We sit in silence for a while until a chilly breeze rolls through and I feel Mel shiver.

"Mother Nature didn't want us to forget it's still winter," Mel says.

"Yeah. Let's get inside where it's warm."

"How about a fire?" I ask when we get inside.

"Yes, please. And that gave me an idea. How about a picnic in front of the fire for dinner tonight?"

"Hmm, do I want to enjoy a picnic in front of the fireplace with a beautiful woman? I'll have to think about it," I joke.

"Dickhead," she says before I hear my favorite giggle.

We go into the library and I set up the puzzle table I bought. Mel grabs one of the jigsaw puzzles she bought. We spend a couple of hours talking and putting the puzzle together. When we finish the puzzle, it's close to dinner-time, so Mel heads into the kitchen.

"I thought we'd do chicken Caesar salad tonight," Mel says.

"Sounds good. Put me to work."

"How about you wash and cut up the lettuce?"

"Yes, ma'am."

Mel cooks the chicken while I get the lettuce ready, then butter the garlic bread. She even makes her own homemade dressing. My kitchen smells delicious, pulling me back to my childhood when my mom always had something in the oven.

"I thought after dinner we could bake cookies together," she says.

"You're amazing, you know that?"

"Thanks, I guess."

"You don't sound sure."

"Sometimes I don't feel amazing."

"Well, to me you are. If anyone else feels different, the hell with them."

Mel looks at her feet and says, "Dinner's ready."

I spread a blanket out on the floor in front of the fireplace. Mel carries two plates of food into the living room while I grab the wine. After pouring us each a glass, we toast and dig into the delicious food she cooked. After we eat, we lay down on the blanket.

"Sweetie, what's wrong?"

"Nothing."

"Come on, you can talk to me."

"I had a run-in with the owner's nephew at work the other day." She tells me what happened and how he spoke to her. My body tenses.

"It's a good thing I wasn't there."

"Jason said the same."

"Just remember, you don't need to put up with that."

"I know. Honestly, I was so shocked that I couldn't speak."

"Promise me if it happens again, you'll report it."

"I promise. Hey, can I ask you something?"

"Are you sure about buying me that horse? It had to be expensive."

"I'm sure."

"Thank you."

"My pleasure. Now, let's get those cookies going."

After the batter's ready, we get the first batch going. Once the last batch is done and cooled, we put the cookies in a container and clean up. Mel looks so damn cute with flour on her clothes and I can't resist her. In my best Cookie Monster voice, I grab her and say, "Me want your cookies."

She laughs and takes off for the bedroom. "Me want cookies," I repeat until I catch her. And damn, her cookies tasted delicious.

The next morning, after breakfast, we take Dave and Maggie for a long ride through the countryside before heading back for another delicious homemade meal. We cuddle on the couch and watch a couple of movies before heading to bed.

CHAPTER 10

Mel

After a very late night, Judd and I sleep in. I'm the first one up, so I get dressed and pad out to the living to order a brunch delivery. A little while later, the doorbell rings. Thinking it's the food, I open the door and stand face to face with Damien and Lexi. Shit.

"You're home early," I say as I feel the heat creeping up my face. "I just stopped by to check on the dogs." And apparently lost my shoes. I hear footsteps behind me.

"Who's at the - oh, hey, guys? Welcome home," Judd says.

Dave and Maggie come running when they hear Damien's voice. After Lexi tells me we'll talk soon, they head home.

"Well, I think they know now," I say.

"I'm surprised they didn't say anything," Judd says.

"If I know Lexi, poor Damien's getting an earful now."

The doorbell rings again. Brunch. "This is why I answered the door. I wanted to surprise you."

"Everything looks delicious, especially you."

I throw my arm across my forehead and say, "My, my, Judd, you're such a sweet talker."

"You're so damn cute."

We spend the rest of the day enjoying each other's company. Judd takes me home after dinner. I need to be on top of my game at work now that Daniel's monitoring me. I'm sitting in my office after lunch when my cell rings. Damien.

"Hello," I say.

"Hey, I'm here with Cassie. Let me put you on speaker. I wanted to talk to you both about a surprise party for Lexi's birthday."

"I'm excited already," I say.

"What did you have in mind?" Cassie asks.

"I wanna do it here. The first part could be before the club opens with just our friends and the staff, then continue when we open with a special karaoke night," Damien says.

"I have a great idea to get her there," I say. "I'll need your help, Cassie."

"Sure, what are ya thinking?" Cassie asks.

"I'll invite her for lunch, telling her that since Damien gets to celebrate her at night, I get lunch. Then you can call her and tell her there's a problem at the club."

"That's perfect," Damien says. "Cassie and Mel, can you work out the details and just let me know? That way I don't get caught. I really want to surprise her."

I hear muffled yelling. "Scott just let me know Lexi's here."

"Mel, I'll call you later," Cassie says and we disconnect.

I spend the rest of the afternoon finishing up my financial reports and getting them loaded into Tableau to present at the next executive meeting. Jay drops by a little before five and we head out together. I'm relieved I didn't have to see Daniel today.

When I get home, I change into jammies and grab myself a bowl of Lucky Charms for dinner. I may be a college-educated executive, but damn, I still love my kid cereals. I'm crunching on the last spoonful of marshmallows when my phone rings and Judd's sexy chest fills my screen. Yep, snuck a picture of him when he was sleeping and I'm not sorry!

"Hey, sexy," I say in my best sultry voice.

"Mmm, hello, my love. I miss you," Judd says.

"I miss you too."

"How was your day?"

"Not bad. I got a lot of work done and managed to avoid the asshole."

"Glad to hear it. I got a call from Damien a little while ago. He let me know you and Cassie are helping him with Lexi's party."

"Yeah. I can't wait. Especially because I get to see you!"

"What are you planning?"

"I'm gonna take her to lunch. Cassie's gonna call and tell us there's an emergency at the club."

"Perfect. Damien filled me in on the rest."

"Promise me no mention of us. I want this day to be all about Lexi."

"You're a good friend, but don't forget you deserve your time in the spotlight too, angel."

"I guess, but not on Lexi's birthday."

"Okay, for now. But, baby, I'm not sure how much longer I can hide us. I love you and I want to tell the world."

"I understand. I'm just not ready. Please understand."

"Okay. Please, just think about it, though."

"I will."

"Good night, my love."

"Good night and sweet dreams."

We disconnect and I sit and stare at my lap. I know Judd's right. What I don't know is why I'm so hesitant. Things are just going so well. I guess I'm afraid I'll jinx it. I grab a book, but I'm too distracted to read, so I turn on the TV and look for some mindless entertainment. I find Dude, Where's My Car starring Ashton Kutcher and Seann William Scott, both of whom I love. I'm at the part where one of the hot female aliens deep throats a popsicle and all I can think about is Judd. My favorite Britny Fox song, In Motion, interrupts my dirty daydream.

I grab my phone and answer. "Hello."

"Hey, Mel. It's Cassie. Just wanted to firm up everything for Saturday."

We spend the next half hour running through everything. Cassie lets me know she'll update Damien and we disconnect. I finish watching the movie and head off to bed. The rest of the work week drags. Jason and I are both spending most of our day in our office, avoiding Daniel. We keep our socializing only on our lunch break and when we're leaving.

Saturday morning arrives and I'm getting ready to do a load of laundry when my washer makes a horrible noise and dies. Shit! I grab my cell and dial Judd.

"Hello, baby," he says when he answers.

"Help!" I exclaim.

"What's wrong?"

"My damn washer just died. Do you know anything about fixing them?"

"On my way."

We disconnect and I take my stuff out of the washer while I wait. I hear his truck pull into the driveway. Peeking out the window, I almost pass out when I see him in jeans, a tight shirt and carrying a toolbox. A million naughty thoughts swirl in my brain. I open the door and my mouth waters when he walks by.

"Good morning, beautiful," he says.

I barely choke out, "Good morning, handsome."

I follow him to my laundry room. Damn, I wanna take a bite out of that sexy ass of his. He grabs his toolbox and gets to work. I wanna grab his tool. Stop it! Behave yourself! But he's so damn sexy. He's here trying to fix your washer. Then he can work on my pipes. Oh my god.

"Earth to Melissa." Judd's voice interrupts my silent argument, and I feel my cheeks redden. "I can only imagine what's going through your pretty little head," he chuckles.

"Guilty. So, what's the verdict?"

"Unfortunately, you need a new washer."

"I had a feeling. Guess I know what I'll be doing tomorrow."

"How about I pick you up? That way, we can load it into my truck and I can hook it up for you."

"You really are my knight, you know that?"

"Why, thank you, Dame Melissa," he says as he bows. "I'm gonna run so you can get ready for lunch."

"Okay, I'll see you tonight."

"Lookin' forward to it."

Judd grabs me and gives me one hell of a kiss. "I'm gonna leave my tools here since I'll need them tomorrow."

"Okay, thanks again. And hey, wear something sexy tonight," I tease.

"Mmm, you too, baby."

After Judd's gone, I finish getting ready and head out to pick Lexi up for lunch.

"You look amazing. Marriage definitely agrees with you," I say.

"Thanks! You, of course, always look amazing," Lexi says.

"If you say so."

"Stop! You're a hottie and you know it, girl! I bet I know at least one cowboy who would agree."

"How many times do I have to tell you? There's nothing going on between Judd and me."

Lexi nods but says nothing. The rest of the drive to lunch is quiet. Once we're inside, I order a bottle of Lexi's favorite wine, Moscato. When the waiter brings it over, I pour us each a glass.

"Happy Birthday to the best friend I could ask for.".

"Thank you," Lexi says.

"Wanna split a ham and cheese calzone?" I ask.

"Sounds good."

"Hey, you okay? You seem down?"

"Nope, all good," Lexi says with a smile. "Calzone sounds perfect."

When our waiter comes back, I order. We're just about finished eating when Lexi's cell rings, but she ignores it. I try to will her to answer. A couple of minutes later, it rings again.

"Sounds like someone needs you," I say.

"They can wait."

When the phone rings a third time, I grab it. "It's Cassie."

"Shit, I better make sure there's not an issue at the club."

"Hey Cass, what's up?"

"Did you try Damien? He can also sign off."

"Okay, I'll be there as soon as I can."

"No problem."

Lexi disconnects and turns to me. "I'm so sorry. Something set off our alarm and I need to go down there."

"No worries, we were done. I'll go pay the check and we can head out."

"Thanks."

We head out to my car after I pay. "Are you sure you're okay?" I ask.

"I was just thinking about the episode of Friends where Rachel found out about Monica and Chandler."

"And that made you sad?"

"Yeah, Monica and Rachel were best friends, but Monica didn't tell her."

"Oh, I get it. Look, there's really nothing to tell."

Lexi lowers her head, her shoulders hunched forward and sighs. "Okay."

I pull into the club's parking lot and see Cassie standing outside with a very handsome police officer.

"Check him out, Mel."

"Damn, he's hot."

"Yeah, and he has cuffs."

"Damn, Damien's made you naughty."

"Thanks for coming," Cassie says.

"No problem," Lexi says.

Cassie opens the door and I hear Lexi gasp when we walk inside. "SURPRISE!"

After Damien walks over and hugs Lexi, the officer takes her to her birthday throne. We watch as he gives her one hell of a birthday strip tease. He's good, but he's not Judd! After the dance, we have dinner. After dinner, Damien wheels out an enormous birthday cake. Once we get the club cleaned up, Cassie opens the doors and the second part of the evening begins.

Damien brings Lexi up on stage, announces her birthday, then the Karaoke contest. Those of us who are friends of Damien and Lexi can't win, but we can still sing. I see Judd whisper something to Lexi. She nods, and he heads up to the stage. Shit. What's he going to do to me this time? I hear the opening notes to Kingdom Come's *What Love Can Be*. Glancing over at Lexi, I see tears sliding down her cheeks and I know I'm going to have to tell her soon.

The rest of the contest is a blur. I try my damnedest not to look at Judd or Lexi. Once they announce the winner, Scott, the club's DJ, opens the dance floor and kicks things off with Steelheart's *I'll Never Let You Go*. I snuggle into Judd's arms and everything around me fades.

"And when do I get to do this for you?" Judd asks.

"Do what?"

"Celebrate your birthday. I just realized I never asked you when it was."

"Today."

"What? Why didn't you say anything?"

"This is Lexi's party."

"But she knows it's your birthday?"

"Yeah."

"And she didn't say anything?"

"It's okay."

"No, it isn't. Is this her actual birthday?"

"No, hers is two days from now, but Damien wanted to do the party on the weekend."

"Happy Birthday, baby. I feel terrible not gettin' you a gift."

"You've already given me everything I need. Except when yours is."

"April twentieth."

"Yay, can't wait!"

"I'm not sure if that's a good or bad thing."

"Depends on your perspective."

"Hmmm."

We keep dancing until Scott announces the last call and security clears the last few people out.

"Do you want me to wait for you?" I ask Lexi.

"I'll ride home with Damien," she says.

"I just need to drop Judd off first," Damien says.

"Um, I'll give him a ride," I say.

"Is that okay?" Damien asks Judd.

"Of course," Judd says and we head out.

As we walk to my car, I say, "You were right."

"About?"

"We need to tell them."

"What changed your mind?"

"Lunch today. Lexi kept hinting, and she was down when I lied and told her there was nothing to tell. I can't stand hurting my friend."

"Forgive me for this, but what about her ignoring your birthday?"

"It's okay. I want her to be happy."

"Well, I want you to be happy."

"I am, thanks to you."

"I promise it will stay that way."

"I know. You've proved it to me again and again. I just need to let go of my past."

"I know that's not easy, but we both need to move forward. Together. Are you in?"

"I'm all in."

We head to Judd's house and I pull into his driveway. "Please stay with me tonight," he begs.

"Nowhere I'd rather be."

He grabs his keys and uses his remote to open the garage. I pull in and park. We head inside and right to bed. And we didn't get a wink of sleep! The next morning, we dragged our sorry asses out of bed and got a new washer for my house. For the next couple of weeks, I was swamped at work and only seeing Judd on the weekend. The weather was finally getting warmer as we approached spring.

One sunny, mild Saturday afternoon, we were out for a ride. As we're driving past the dog park, I look over and see Dave and Maggie running around, while Damien and Lexi watch from a bench.

"Let's do it," I exclaim.

"Now?"

"Why not?"

Judd smiles and pulls into the parking lot. He walks around, opens my door, and helps me out of his truck. He takes my hand in his as we approach the gate to the park. Lexi watches us, tears spilling out of her eyes. When we get to the bench, she jumps up and nearly knocks me on my ass with a hug.

"Tryin' to channel your inner-Dave?" I tease.

"I'm so happy for you. I can't even be mad you kept it from me."

"What?"

"Come on, I know you've been together for a while. So, when?"

I pull Lexi away from the guys. "After the Halloween party."

"I knew that costume was hot. Now, I want details. How big's his dick?"

"Lexi, honestly."

"Come on, girl, I need deets."

"Well, you're not getting them from me."

"Fine. Seriously, though, nobody deserves this more than you."

"Thanks. I'm sorry I kept it from you."

"Can I ask why?"

"You know my past. I was so scared that if I told you, I would jinx it."

"I get it." She gives me another huge hug and we rejoin the guys.

"I was just telling Judd that we need to go celebrate," Damien says.

"Ooh, good idea. I'll call the other girls," Lexi says. My stomach churns and I lean into Judd.

"Let us know," Judd says.

Damien shakes his hand as Lexi gives me one more hug. Once we're in Judd's truck, he says, "What's wrong?"

"I wish it wasn't a whole group outing."

"I know. We could get out of it."

"I can't do that to Lexi."

"Well, then we'll make an early exit."

I nod, but say nothing. Lexi calls that evening to let us know we're all going to meet at Palermo's Pizzeria tonight. At least I won't have a lot of time to freak myself out. As we're approaching the restaurant, Judd says, "I could keep going."

"You're sweet."

Everyone else is already there when we arrive. They watch us walk in, and I feel butterflies in my stomach. I'm really not a big fan of being the center of attention like this. I love being the center of Judd's world when we're alone, but not in group settings. Turns out, I had nothing to worry about. Lexi was so engrossed in a conversation with the other rockstar wives, she didn't even look up when Judd and I sat down.

When our waiter comes to take our order, Damien says, "Four large pies, two plain and two pepperoni."

"And a grilled chicken Caesar salad please," I add.

97

"Two of those, please," Judd says.

Lexi finally looks up and says, "Oh, hey, when did you two arrive?"

"Just got here," I say.

"Cool," Lexi says without even a mention of why we're supposedly here. I look down at my lap as I fight back tears. Judd gives my hand a light squeeze and I feel a little better.

"I'm gonna go to the ladies' room," I whisper to Judd and he nods.

"Hey, Mel," I hear when I get inside.

"Hi, Tammy," I say with a smile.

"You okay?"

"I guess."

"I'm a waitress. I'm good at listening," she says.

"Well, we, Judd and me, finally told our friends that we were together. This was supposed to be a celebratory dinner, but she's so wrapped up with the other girls, she hardly even acknowledged me."

"Aw, I'm sorry. That sucks."

"It really does. I love that she found what she always wanted, but I don't think I fit into her world anymore."

"Sometimes people grow apart. I should know."

"I'm sorry."

"Thanks. But, hey, if you ever need an ear, give me a shout."

"Thanks."

Tammy grabs a piece of paper out of her handbag and gives me her number. I tear half of the paper off and give her mine. We walk out together, and I'm feeling even better. She gives Judd a wave as she heads to her table. Our food arrives, along with a couple of bottles of wine. Damien pours everyone a glass and passes them around.

"A toast to our newest couple, Judd and Mel," Damien says.

The other guys all say cheers and clink glasses, but Lexi keeps talking until Damien clears his throat.

"Congrat -" Alex says before she's interrupted.

"I was talking," Lexi says. "We were finalizing plans for our girls' trip on Monday. Uh, we would have invited you, Mel, but we figured you'd have to work. It's nice not having to work a nine-to-five anymore." She takes a sip of wine without even clinking glasses with me as the other girls stare at her.

"I'm proud of what I've accomplished in my career," I say.

"Oh, well, I'm glad for you," Lexi replies. I feel my eyes welling up again.

"Can we just go?" I whisper in Judd's ear.

"Sure. One sec." I watch Judd walk up to the counter, ask for to-go boxes and pay for our part of the meal. He packs up our salads, then we get up. Damien apologizes and Judd nods. He takes my hand in his as we walk to the door. As soon as we're in his truck, my eyes spill.

"I'm so sorry, sweetie," Judd says, as he caresses my face.

"Can I stay at your house tonight? I need to be in your arms."

"Of course, my angel."

CHAPTER 11
Judd

Monday morning, I'm working out in the yard when Damien walks over.

"I'm sorry about the other night," he says.

"Mel was really hurt."

"Well, Lexi was hurt that Mel kept it from her."

"I get that, but she could have said something at the dog park, instead of doing that in front of everyone."

"You're right. I told her on the way home I wasn't happy about how she acted."

"All good, man, but I think we'll hold off on joining any more group outings, at least for now."

"Please don't. We love having you there. Lexi really is happy for Mel, it was just a reaction to being hurt."

"I'm willing to put it behind me this time, but if it happens again-"

"It won't."

"Good."

After Damien leaves, I finish planting a flower garden as a surprise for Mel, I hop into a shower and head down to the local furniture store to buy a bed for the loft.

When I get home, I get the bed setup and put on the black satin sheets I bought. I get dinner prepped and wait for my sweetheart to get home. While she's in the shower, I pack dinner and a bottle of wine into a picnic basket. She comes down when she's done, a smile appearing on her face when she sees the basket.

"Are we going to the park for a picnic?"

"Yes, to the picnic, but not at the park. Come with me."

I put an arm around her and we walk out to the barn. I made sure the door to the loft was closed so she couldn't see my second surprise. We get to the back of the barn, leading to the backyard.

"Take my hand and close your eyes," I say. I walk her to the garden I planted today. "You can open your eyes now."

She squeals when she sees what I did.

"Oh, Judd, this is amazing. I love the little bistro table and chairs. And, wow, an entire garden full of marigolds."

"I saw the picture of you as a child near a garden, a look of joy on your face."

"That was my grandma's house. It was my sanctuary, especially when things got bad with my parents. Thank you so much for this. I'm officially naming this The Bistro."

"Anything for the love of my life."

The weather tonight is perfect for dining outside. We laugh and talk, as we enjoy homemade chicken sandwiches, potato salad, and wine. After we finish dinner, I pack up the basket and walk her back to the barn.

"And now for my second surprise."

We walk up the stairs leading to the loft. Before I open the door, I have her close her eyes again. I open the door and walk her inside.

"Okay, you can open them."

"Oh my god, Judd."

"Do you like it?"

"No. I love it."

"I'm so glad, because we're sleeping here tonight."

"I have a feeling we won't be doing much sleeping."

"Not if I can help it, baby."

I pull her into my arms and kiss her. She opens for me, and I deepen the kiss as our tongues intertwine. My dick responds with a vengeance, and all I can focus on is getting her naked. I slide my hands under her shirt, caressing her soft skin as I lift the shirt off of her, followed by her bra. She removes my shirt and I pull her against me. I love the feeling of her skin on mine.

"So beautiful, my love."

"Oh, Judd. I love you."

"I love you, baby."

We finish undressing each other. I take her hand and lead her to the bed, then pull the covers down.

"Mmm, I love the sheets," Mel purrs.

"Please come lay with me."

Pulling her tight against me, I crush my lips to hers. I love how she opens for me every single time. My tongue finds hers and she moans into my mouth. I can't get enough of this amazing angel. I pull her to her side and run my hands down her back, then her sexy little ass. Rolling her onto her back, I move on top of her, sucking her neck before running my tongue down her throat and between her breasts.

I crave her taste, so I run my tongue down her sexy stomach until I'm where she wants me most. I swipe my tongue between her folds and she bucks off the bed. I lick her at a feverish pace and she quickly comes undone.

"On your back. Now! I need to taste your delicious cock."

I lay down and watch as she gets on all fours and crawls over to me. Fuck, this woman is so damn sexy. She straddles me, wraps her pretty mouth around my cock. She lifts her eyes and locks them with mine while she sucks me off. She stops to suck on my balls and it feels so fucking good. Her mouth returns to my cock. I growl as I come down her sexy throat. She slides her body up against mine and I'm hard again.

"Mmm, haven't had enough, my sexy cowboy? Looks like I need to take a ride."

"Oh, woman, please. I need to be inside you."

I watch her grab my dick and line it up with her sweet pussy. She lowers herself slowly and I swear to fuck it feels better every single time she's wrapped around me. I'm as deep inside of her as I can as she rolls her hips.

"Oh, my sweet Melissa, you feel so damn good. I love watching you ride me, my dirty little cowgirl."

She leans back, bracing her hands on my thighs. She bounces up and down on top of me while my fingers find her clit. I stroke her fast as she rides, screaming as she drenches my cock.

"Uh oh, I've been a naughty girl, soaking you like that." She climbs off and lays across my legs. "Please, Judd, please spank my ass."

"On your knees. Hold on to the headboard. Now!"

She complies and wiggles her ass for me. I swat her ass, and she moans. "Mmm, feels so good."

"Quiet."

I spank her a few more times. She moans softly.

"Spread those sexy legs for me."

She does as she's told. "Good girl. Now you get a reward."

"Mmm."

I slide my fingers inside her pussy and stroke her G-spot hard. She quickly explodes and squirts all over my hand. I don't stop. She squirts over and over, her screams filling the room. Her entire body quakes as I keep stroking.

"Have you had enough?"

"No. More, please."

Damn, this woman. I stroke harder and her breathing matches my pace.

"Your pussy's so fucking wet. I wanna taste you this time." I lay between her legs. Claiming her pussy with my mouth, I slide my tongue inside and lick her hard while she writhes on my face. "Come for me, baby. NOW! I need to drink you." She covers my face, and fuck, she tastes so sweet.

"How's that pussy feel?"

"So good."

"But can you take more?"

"I can take as much as you can give."

"That's my good little cowgirl. I want you on all fours holding the headboard so I can fuck that sweet pussy. I'm gonna pound you like never before. But first, I want you to beg for it."

"Oh, please, Judd. Please, my sexy cowboy. I need your huge cock inside my pussy. I can't take another second without my pussy being pounded."

I grab my cock and line it up with her slit. She's so fucking wet that I slide in easily. I thrust in and out of her harder than I've ever done, my balls slapping her ass as I pound her.

"Oh, Judd. Spank me, please," she screams. Her ass is a dark pink by the time I empty inside of her. She can't possibly handle anything else. I was wrong.

She rolls onto her back and spreads her legs as wide as she can. "My pussy needs more punishment."

"Tell me what you want. And it better be damn hot."

She hesitates for a minute.

"Tell me now, or I get dressed. I wanna know what you want."

"I want you to watch me get myself off."

Oh fuck. My dick hardens. I watch as she takes her hands and spreads her pussy wide open. She throws her head back and rubs her clit as she moans. She stops and flashes me the naughtiest damn smile I've ever seen. "Now, I want you to suck my clit."

Her body quakes as she quickly explodes. She emits a long sigh as she comes down.

"Um, we might not be sleeping here after all," she whispers.

"I brought an extra set of sheets when I put the bed in."

"My sexy cowboy thinks of everything! But what about getting ready for bed?"

"Go through that door."

She peeks inside and sees a half-bathroom, freshly decorated and complete with the necessary toiletries.

"You really are the perfect man."

"I'm far from perfect."

"Well, you're perfect for me."

I walk over and kiss the top of her head. "Let's get ready for bed. I'm exhausted."

"Hmm, cowboy can't hang with his dirty cowgirl?" she teases.

"Oh, it's like that, huh?"

She sticks her tongue out as she races into the bathroom. When we're both finished, we crawl into bed, still naked, and I pull her close. Taking a deep breath then exhaling, I say, "I need to tell you somethin'."

"What's up?"

"I saw Lexi and Damien earlier. She wasn't at all sorry for the other night."

"Well, maybe she's going through something?"

"You're too sweet."

"Maybe, but I'm not willing to just throw in the towel. I wanna have a chance to talk to her first."

I nod and kiss her forehead. She yawns and nestles into my chest and she's out cold. I turn the light off and drift off to the sound of her breathing.

I wake up to the sound of her on the phone. "Yes, thanks, I'll be sure to rest."

"Um, naughty girl, did you just pretend to be sick?"

"I may have," she giggles.

"Good, because I have a surprise for you, baby. Get dressed," I say.

"Ooh, I'm so excited. Where are we going?"

"You'll find out when we get there."

After we grab breakfast at our favorite diner, I head to my next destination. She squeals when I pull into the parking lot of A and H Harness and Tack Company. We get everything she'll need to ride and head back to my ranch. I show her how to get JoJo ready to ride. I get Rex ready and help Mel mount JoJo. After I mount Rex, we head out to the riding ring.

"I know it's been a while since you've ridden. Do you need any help?" I ask.

I look over at Mel and the look of pure joy on her face warms my heart. "Thank you, but I'm fine."

I can't take my eyes off of her beautiful blonde hair flowing behind her as she gallops around the ring. I swear I've never seen a more beautiful sight. I take Rex outside of the ring and just watch her. She rides for almost an hour before she realizes she's alone in the ring. She slows JoJo to a trot and walks over to me.

"What happened?" she asks.

"Just wanted to watch you ride, darlin'. The joy on your face was mesmerizing."

"I've never felt so free. Well, except for the night with the video. Thank you!"

"I'm happy you feel so comfortable. I want this to feel like home."

"I want this to be home," she whispers as her eyes glisten.

"What?"

"I'm sorry, was that too forward?"

"No, not at all. Do you really want to live here with me?"

"Yeah. I don't wanna spend any more nights alone."

I ride into the ring and stop next to her. I lean over and kiss her. Out of the corner of my eye, I see JoJo nuzzle Rex. I break our kiss and say, "See, even they approve."

"I'm scared," she says.

"Baby, if this is too fast-"

"No. What I mean is, I'm scared this is all a dream that I don't wanna wake up from."

"I could pinch you if you want."

"Mmm, yes, please," she says with a giggle.

"I'll go tomorrow while you're at work and get boxes."

"I won't need many right now. I only have to pack my clothes."

"What about the rest of your stuff?"

"Oh, I couldn't bring all that here. This is your home."

"It's our home now, baby. I want pieces of you here."

"Are you sure?"

"Yeah. I don't want even one more minute of my life to be without you in it."

"What if you get sick of me?"

"Not possible. Besides, I have unused rooms, so I was thinkin' we could designate one room each to be just ours."

"I get my very own Bitch Barn?"

"And I get a Dickhead Den."

We crack up laughing as we trot back to the stables. We dismount and get the horses situated before we head back inside.

"I wanna celebrate. The Moon is having a disco night on Saturday. You up for it?" I ask.

"You bet I am. I have a secret soft spot for The Bee Gees."

"Don't tell anyone but me, too."

"Oh my god, we need to go as Tony and Stephanie from *Saturday Night Fever.*"

"You really think I can pull off the white suit?"

"Babe, if Dwayne 'The Rock' Johnson could do it, so can you!"

"It's a date."

"I can't wait!"

CHAPTER 12
Mel

I'm sitting at work the next morning, getting caught up on emails, when Jason pops his head in my doorway.

"You busy?" Jason asks.

"Just catching up on emails. Come in. Is something wrong?"

"King Dick was on a rampage yesterday about you missing work."

"Shit. What did he say?"

"I think he's after your job."

"They can't fire me for taking a sick day."

"No, but I feel like he's up to something, so just be careful."

"Great, and I was in a good mood when I got here. But thanks for letting me know."

"I always got you, girl. Now, dish on the good mood."

I smile just thinking about it. "I'm moving in with Judd."

"Wow, that's huge."

I'm about to respond when my desk phone buzzes. "Yes, Allie."

"Danger," she says.

"Shit." Just then, a silhouette fills the room as Daniel appears in the doorway.

"Thanks for showing me those tips to organize my email."

"You're welcome. If you run into anything else, let me know," Jason says as he gets up.

"Will do. Good morning, Daniel, can I help you?"

"Please," he sneers. "You're just some worthless woman. Nothing you could do for me."

I count to ten so I don't lose my job. "Worthless? Then why have I been promoted several times?"

"I don't know."

"Then go ask your uncle. Now, if there's nothing I can do for you, I need to get back to work."

"As if you know what work is."

"Have the day you deserve, Daniel."

He turns and stomps out. Spoiled fucking brat. After documenting the encounter, I sit and silently practice the speech I plan on giving him if he gets his way. I'm not even sure I'd be completely disappointed at this point. I've given this place my all, but that was because I was alone and it kept me occupied. Being with Judd, though, has changed my perspective on some things. I see Allie and Jason come walking in.

"Are you okay?" Allie asks.

I nod and grab a piece of paper. Lunch at Chili's? They both nod yes and head out. I spend the rest of the morning focusing on my emails and a couple of reports until my lunch dates appear. The Chili's is right across the parking lot, so we walk over together. Once we're seated, I say, "I don't know how much more of that asshat I can take."

"I really think he's trying to get rid of you," Jason says.

"Me too and if he does, I'm going too," Allie adds.

"Please don't do that. You're so good at your job and you have a lot of potential to move up," I say.

"But if he takes over your job, I won't be able to work for him," she says.

"I'd make sure that wouldn't happen, but no worries, as he doesn't have a leg to stand on," Jason says.

"Leaving wouldn't be the end of the world," I say.

"But you love your job," Jason says.

"I do, but it's not my whole life," I say.

"Ah, so it's what I thought," Jason says.

"Ooh, the handsome cowboy?" Allie asks.

"Since I've been with him, I'm just not sure I wanna be stuck working in an office anymore."

"So, what do you want to do?" Jason asks.

"Help at the ranch," I say.

"Does he work without a shirt on?" Allie asks as she sighs.

"Allison!" I tease. "You already have a man! Speaking of which, I'd love to meet him. How would you both, and you too, Jason, join us on Saturday night?"

"What's Saturday night?" Allie asks.

"The Full Moon Saloon is having Disco Night. Judd and I are going to celebrate me moving in with him."

"Excuse me," Jason exclaims. "You waited half a damn day to tell me that?"

"Sorry," I say, unable to wipe the smile off my face.

"Well, despite being pissed at you for not telling me, I'll be there!" Jason says.

"Us too," Allie adds.

"Yay! I'm so glad," I say, clapping.

We all laugh our way through burgers, fries and diet sodas, and I feel much better. The rest of the day goes by pretty quickly, and before I know it I'm pulling into Judd's driveway. Our driveway. He's sitting on the front porch and damn, he looks so sexy.

"Welcome home, my beautiful goddess," he says, and my insides melt.

"Damn, you're a sight for sore eyes."

As I approach the house, the most delicious smell fills my nose. Marinara sauce and garlic bread hang heavy in the air.

"What did you do?" I ask as my tummy rumbles.

"Baked stuffed shells, a Caesar salad, and garlic bread. Why don't you get changed and meet me down at The Bistro."

"It'll be my pleasure."

"First, though, I have a surprise for you." Judd grabs my hand and walks me to the bathroom. I can't believe what I see on the wall.

"When did you do this?"

"Today."

110

"Thank you so much," I say as I stand there looking at my rubber duck collection displayed on shelves in the bathroom.

"Anything for you, love. I'll see you out back."

After returning to our bedroom, I gratefully shed my work skin, opting for a pair of jeans and a low-cut tee. What! Gotta keep that sexy cowboy thirsty. I love the feeling of the grass on my bare feet as I join my dinner companion for some lovely garden dining. Judd stands behind my chair, pushing me in once I sit. He sits across from me and pours two glasses of Moscato. After a toast to my moving in, we eat the delicious food he prepared. We sit and talk for a while after dinner, mostly because I can't move from how full I am.

"What did I do to deserve someone like you?" I ask.

"Sweetheart, one of the first things I figured out about you was your giving heart. What also became apparent was the way people've taken advantage of your generosity. Now, it's your turn to be taken care of."

"But -"

"Nope, no buts, unless it's your cute little butt. Which, by the way, looks delectable in those jeans."

"Don't get me started about how you look in your jeans. Though I do prefer you out of them."

"Keep that up, Little Miss Naughty, and I won't be such a gentleman."

"Promise?"

He flashes me a wicked smile that sends lava flowing through my veins. Next thing I know, I'm over his shoulder, heading toward the barn. He carries me up to the loft and reminds me that the only thing more fun than riding a horse is riding a cowboy.

The rest of the week, we have a quick dinner each night, then head over to my house to pack. The more time I spend at the ranch, the less I want to keep going into an office to work. If only. Yeah, well, suck it up, buttercup. Mmm, though, to watch Judd work those muscles all day. Holy shit. I feel my panties dampen at the mere thought of his tan skin glistening with sweat, his musky scent, those abs, that ass. That delicious fucking everything-I-ever-wanted hunk of a man.

"Earth to Melissa." Judd's sexy voice brings me back to reality.

"Sorry, just thinking about how much stuff I have to pack."

"Oh, is that so? Then why did I hear a couple of moans escape your pretty mouth?"

Heat rises in my cheeks as I giggle. "Okay, you caught me."

"Well, what are you waiting for? I wanna know what you were really thinkin' about."

"Um, I was picturing you working on your ranch, shirtless."

"That's it?"

"Uh, well, no. Your tanned, sweat-soaked skin was gleaming in the sun. All I could think about was licking your abs."

He pulls me close and gives me a kiss that could melt Antarctica.

"So, what had you thinkin' about that?"

"I'm not sure I wanna spend the rest of my life working in an office."

"What would you do instead?"

"Something outdoors, at least in the nice weather."

"But you love your job."

"I do, but I'm not sure it loves me anymore."

"Is that little jackass giving you trouble again?"

"Jay thinks he might be trying to get rid of me."

"I hope he's wrong, but I promise you, if anything does happen, we'll figure it out."

"Thanks, baby."

"Anything for my girl."

We finish up and head home, with plans to come back in the morning. As we're riding back to the ranch, Judd asks, "What are you thinking about doin' with your house?"

"I'm not sure, but I guess selling makes the most sense."

"Maybe, but let's wait a bit."

"But I want to give that to you since I'm taking over part of your house."

"First, it's our house now. And second, absolutely not, my love."

"But I wanna contribute."

"Fine. Then keep filling my life with your love, laughter, and companionship."

"And what will you fill me with?"

"I do believe I've already shown you that."

"Mmm, and I sure do love seeing it."

He shakes his head as a hearty laughter escapes him. Damn, I love this man so much. Saturday morning, we finish packing the things I want to keep at my new house. The rest, we'll decide on later. After a hot, steamy shower together, we get ready for disco night. When I see Judd in his white suit, I almost pass out cold. Since my dress is white, I grab a white lace lingerie set out of my drawer.

"My beautiful, sexy angel. This would make a stunning picture," Judd says.

"Then take one." What the hell did I just say? Well, you made a sex tape with him. Yeah, but I was disorientated by my desire. So? This is different. No, it's not. You know you can trust him. Fine.

"Are you sure?"

"Yeah."

"Please, lie down on the bed."

I lay on my side, using my arm to prop my head up. I put my other hand on my hip and gaze at my sexy cowboy. He grabs his phone and snaps a couple of pictures, then shows me. I've never been that girl who was confident about her looks, but damn, I look good. I finish getting ready and we head out. I don't know exactly what this man's done to me, but I like it.

"Can I tell you something?" I ask.

"Of course, honey."

"Thank you for helping me find me."

"What do ya mean?"

"I never would've let someone take a picture like that. And, when you showed me, I actually liked how I look. You did that."

"My goddess deserves to be worshiped."

"Mmm, you do that very well. But for tonight, I can't wait to hit the dance floor!"

"Me either. And that's something I need to thank you for. I was never one for dancing until you."

"Well, you look damn good doing it, cowboy!"

We get inside and see Tammy. "You two look awesome," she gushes.

"Thanks, girl, so do you," I say.

"Anyone joining you two tonight?" Tammy asks.

"Yeah, three or four," Judd answers.

"Follow me," she says, as she leads us to one of the bigger tables.

Jay and Allie both text me, and I let them know where we're sitting. Jay gets there first and I can't help but notice Tammy looking him up and down.

"Well, if you two aren't the disco king and queen, I dunno who is," Jay teases.

"Shut it, dork," I say.

"Seriously, though, you both look amazing," Jay says.

"Oh wow, check out Allie," I say, nodding their way.

"Hey Mel. Hey Jason. This is my boyfriend Dane," Allie says. "Dane, this is Jason and Mel from work, and Mel's boyfriend, Judd."

"Nice to meet you all," Dane says.

Tammy makes her way over. "What can I get everyone? Beer and Moscato for you two?" She asks, pointing to Judd and me.

"You got it," I say.

"Moscato for me too, please," Allie says.

"Beer, please," Jay says.

Dane rounds out the group, ordering a beer. Judd orders a bunch of appetizers to share. We all chat, getting to know each other while we wait for our order. I lean over to Jay and whisper, "Tammy was checkin' you out."

"She's cute," he says and for the first time, I see a gleam in his eyes. As good of friends as we are, there are some parts of himself that he holds close to the vest. I've always suspected a woman destroyed his heart once. Maybe Tammy could be the one to fix him. As if on cue, Tammy appears with our drinks. Her hand brushes Jay's hand when she hands him his beer and the look they exchanged was unmistakable. Tammy blushes and quickly takes off toward the bar. When she returns with our food, she steals a quick glance at Jay but doesn't say a word.

As we're eating, the music stops and the bar's owner, Nick, walks on stage. "Hey all. Thanks for coming out. We have a special treat for you tonight. Hope ya'll brought your dancin' shoes, 'cause we're having a contest. And we have a special judge, Miss Doriana Sanchez.

"Oh my god, I love her," I squeal. "How the hell am I gonna dance in front of her?"

114

"You're gonna be amazing sweetheart," Judd says.

After announcing the rules, the DJ kicks off the contest and Judd pulls me to the dance floor.

"Someone's a bit eager," I tease.

"I want everyone to see my sexy disco momma," Judd says. Allie and Dane join us, but Jay stays at the table. I feel a pang that he's by himself when I see Tammy approach the table. She's says something that puts a smile on his face and I see them walking toward us. I can't help but notice they look great together. Doriana and Nick circle the dance floor, eliminating couples one by one.

The contest gets down to five couples, including Judd and me when we hear *Stayin' Alive* start.

"Time to win this thing," Judd says.

"My, my, I like this side of you."

We do our best to impersonate Tony and Stephanie's dance from Saturday Night Fever and when I see Judd emulate John Travolta's famous pose, I lose it. He looks so damn sexy. My panties are soaked. Allie and Dane get eliminated along with two more couples, leaving just Judd and me, along with one other couple. When the song ends, the DJ stops the music. Nick grabs the microphone and walks between us and the other couple.

"We have our winner. Doriana, please do the honors," Nick announces.

Doriana grabs Judd's and my wrist and raises them. She hands us a trophy as we hear applause fill the room. "Presenting the disco king and queen, our champions, Judd and Melissa," Doriana says. We get our picture taken with her, then head back to our table.

"Damn, girl," Jay says.

"I can't believe it," I squeal.

"That was so much fun," Judd says and plants a toe-curling kiss on my lips. I barely notice the whistles from our friends as everything but Judd disappears. Tangling my tongue with his, I leave him no doubt what I want to do when we get home.

He grabs the trophy with one hand, me with the other hand, and we race to the parking lot. We don't get out of bed until almost noon the next day. And, no, we didn't spend that time sleeping!

CHAPTER 13

Judd

I hear Mel pull into the garage and when she comes inside, my eyes go wide. Her ponytail is halfway out and her blouse is untucked. I already know the answer, but ask anyway. "Tough day?"

Flopping down on the couch, she sighs loudly and says, "Daniel."

"Enough said. And I have a perfect solution. Go get changed while I get things ready."

She trudges into the bedroom and returns a few minutes later in jeans and a KISS t-shirt. Damn, she's so cute! I hand Mel her hat and she flashes a bright smile. "How did you know exactly what I need?"

"You're my soulmate. I'll always know, my love." I grab the picnic basket off the table and we head out to the garage. We load up our fishing gear and head to the park. Nobody's at the dock, so we set up there.

Mel grabs a sandwich and a bottle of water out of the basket. "Peanut butter and jelly, my favorite!"

After we eat, we sit quietly, watching the water as we fish. Today's one of those perfect spring days. The temperature's in the low seventies and there's not a cloud in the sky, and a light breeze comes off the lake. I look over and see Mel gazing out at the water, a look of peace on her face. The tip of her rod bends.

"Babe, you're gettin' a bite," I say.

She looks down, placing her hands over the rod. She grabs her rod and gives it a sharp tug, then reels. She pulls the biggest bass I've ever seen out of the water and her face lights up.

"Damn, girl! Nice catch!"

"Thanks!"

I'm about to offer her help, but she grabs a rag, gets her fish off of the hook and releases it back into the pond. Nothin' hotter than a woman who knows what she's doing.

"You sure know how to handle a rod," I say.

"And don't you ever forget it, baby," she says with a wink.

We keep fishing until we use up all the bait and I'm proud to say my woman out-fished me.

"I'm gonna run the stuff to the truck. Be right back," I say. As I'm heading back to the dock, I see Damien and Lexi. Mel stands up and I see Lexi say something to her. Mel drops her head, staring at her feet, so I rush down.

"Hey guys, what's up?" I ask.

Lexi snickers and I see Mel's head whip up. "What did I do to you?" Mel asks Lexi.

"What do ya mean?"

"First, the night of our celebration, then your comment tonight."

"Not my fault you're boring."

"What exactly makes me boring?"

"Shit like this."

"I happen to enjoy fishing."

"Since when?"

"I always have, but it was never something you were interested in, so I always did it alone. Now, I'm lucky that I don't have to."

"Whatever. Let's go, Damien."

"I think you owe Mel an apology first," Damien says.

"Yeah, whatever, sorry," Lexi says.

"All good," Mel says. She sits back down on the dock.

"Wait here," I say to Mel. "Damien, wait up."

I hear Lexi say, "I'll be in the damn car. Hurry up."

"What's up?" Damien asks me.

"I'm not thrilled with the way Lexi's been treating Mel. What's goin' on?"

Damien lets out a loud sigh. "I wish I knew. Her mood's been all over the place lately. The other guys have all said something, and I'm running out of excuses."

"I'm sorry, man. I don't wanna add to your troubles, but Mel is my priority."

"I understand. I'm hesitant to ask, but do you think Mel could try talking to her?"

"I'll ask her, best I can do."

"Thanks, man." I hear Lexi laying on the horn. "You better go."

Damien nods and races off, and I head back to the pond and sit down next to my girl. "What did Damien have to say?" Mel asks.

"Lexi's mood's been all over the place. He was wonderin' if you'd try talking to her. Told him I'd ask."

"I wonder if she's going through 'the change.' I promise I'll try."

"You're a good friend."

"Thanks. Wish I felt like it."

I wrap my arm around her and she lays her head on my shoulder. We sit quietly and gaze at the reflection of the sun as it sets. The view is stunning, made even better by the beauty sitting next to me.

"I love you," I hear her whisper.

I look over and she's gazing at me. "I love you more," I say before laying a tender kiss on her pretty mouth. She opens for me and I tease her tongue with mine. She moans into my mouth. We sit there kissing for a gloriously long time as the breeze from the water increases. I feel Mel shiver and I wrap her tighter in my arms.

We finally come up for air and Mel says, "Dance with me."

I stand, help her up, and pull her into my arms. "We need music," she whispers.

Rather than grab my cell, I sing to her as she nestles into me. As we slowly sway to my song, she joins me. Standing here in each other's arms, singing together, is sublime. We finish the song and just stand, gazing at each other. "Baby, you look even more beautiful in the moonlight," I say.

"There's just something about the full moon," Mel says.

"There's just something about you."

"Oh, Judd. I, um, never mind."

"What, baby. Tell me."

"I've always wanted to make love outside."

"Come with me." I walk her to the grass next to the dock and lay her down. We spend the next hour passionately loving each other under the moonlit sky. We're lying together afterward when Mel says, "Thank you for tonight. And not just this. Relaxing at the park is exactly what I needed."

"Honey, if the stress of that job, or more like Daniel, gets to be too much, we'll figure things out."

"Just knowing that helps. And I promise, I'll tell you."

"That's my angel. Now, we better get dressed before someone catches us."

"Let 'em," she jokes. "We look damn good doing this."

"Hmm, maybe I should have said that's my little devil."

She laughs for the whole walk back to the truck. I'm glad to see her more relaxed than when she came home. After we unload the truck, we go sit on the couch before we get ready for bed.

"So, I've been thinking about something," Mel says as we're driving home.

"Oh yeah, what?"

"What I could do on the ranch if I did leave my job."

"And what did you come up with?"

"What if we started adding baked goods to what we sell? Not just sweets, but also breads and stuff. Or even packaged healthy meals."

"That's always somethin' I've thought about, especially after having a mom who baked all the time. I just knew I couldn't do it alone. But now, with you, anything's possible."

"Life really is incredible when you have the right partner."

I'm about to respond when Mel's cell rings. I hear a loud sigh when she looks at the screen.

"Hello."

"And what do you want me to do about it?"

"She's your daughter."

"She's never been a sister to me."

119

"Yeah, well, I'm not a bank. There are plenty of places hiring."

"Not my problem."

"Goodbye."

Mel disconnects, and an even louder sigh fills my ears.

"What did Trish do now?" I ask.

"Trish's car died and she can't afford the repair bill. So, Mom thought I should pay."

"Why? She's an adult."

"Exactly. Not my fault that she blows every paycheck as soon as she gets it."

"I hate that they keep putting this stuff on you. Especially after the way she treated you."

"And they expect me to just pay it, not even make it a loan. I tried that once and when they refused, I took my checkbook and went home."

"Good for you."

"The thing is, I'm not trying to be bitchy, but I worked for that money, not her."

"Right. She's not your responsibility. And I will always have your back where that's concerned."

"Thanks. It helps having someone to talk to about it. I used to let her walk all over me, but I finally found the strength to stand up for myself."

"Can I ask how? And it's okay if you tell me no."

"I'm not ashamed. I was really in a low place after Derek. Probably the lowest I'd ever been. One morning, I decided I'd had enough of feeling like shit. So I started seeing a therapist. I've never told a soul before today."

"How come?"

"There's still some who view asking for help as a weakness. For me, it's the opposite. I felt strong for the first time in a long time when I walked into that office. And I only got stronger from there."

"I understand. My dad always tried to convince me that vulnerability equaled weakness."

"He was wrong. Do you know the exact moment I fell in love with you?"

"Halloween?"

"No. I liked you from the first moment I met you, and I grew to love you, but I didn't truly fall in love with you until you told me about your mom. That you trusted me with something so painful, so personal, showed me how you felt about me. At that moment, I knew you were the one."

"My sweet Melissa."

After a big yawn, she says, "I'm exhausted."

Scooping her up, I carry her to the bathroom. By the time I'm finished, she's already curled up, sound asleep. I nestle in next to her, kiss her forehead and whisper, "Mine. Forever."

* * *

Friday finally arrives, and the weather is gorgeous. The sun shines bright and the temperature is a comfortable seventy degrees. I spend the morning getting a fun surprise ready for my goddess. I'm excited when I see her pull into the driveway around noon.

"Welcome home, baby. Hurry and grab a shower. I have a surprise for you," I say.

"Tell me!"

"No way. You'll find out in due time, my love."

She sticks her tongue out at me, then takes off laughing. Chasing after her, I call out, "You're in trouble for that."

"Only if you catch me."

I catch up to her, put her over my shoulder, and put her in the shower stall fully clothed. Her eyes go wide when she sees my hand on the faucet. "You wouldn't dare," she says.

"Oh, I wouldn't?"

I turn on the water and soak her. But instead of getting mad, she laughs as she peels her clothes off. She takes her ponytail holder out and her beautiful blonde hair falls to her shoulders. I watch as she washes herself, my dick stirring as she lathers up her sexy skin. Seeing her hands running over her body is almost too much for me. But there will be plenty of time for that later.

When Mel's done, I hand her a towel and help her out of the

shower. She finishes getting ready and we head out. When we hit the Northeast Extension, she squeals. "Please tell me we're going to the Poconos."

"Yeah. I rented a cabin for the weekend."

"Yay! I'm so excited. I love camping!"

"Then this is gonna be a fun weekend."

When we pull up in front of the cabin, Mel leans over and kisses my cheek. "There are no other cabins around."

"Exactly why I booked this one."

"You're the best."

"No, we are, baby."

It's nearing dinnertime when we get everything unloaded, so I go outside and build a fire in the fire ring.

"How does hot dogs for dinner and s'mores for dessert sound?" I ask.

"Sounds perfect."

"I'll be right back," I say after we finish eating. Mel smiles when she sees the guitar case.

"I didn't know you had that," Mel says.

"Just bought it today." I strum *Forever* by KISS. She gazes at me while I sing to her, the softest smile on her beautiful face.

"You're so talented," she says when I finish.

"Thanks, baby. Your love inspires me."

"I love you. And I love that you brought me here. It's beautiful."

"Just wait until tomorrow. There's a gorgeous lake about a mile walk from here. I thought we could pack a picnic lunch and do some fishing."

"That sounds perfect. But what about tonight?"

"Oh, I have plans for tonight, too."

"I sure hope they involve us getting naked."

"Oh, yes, they definitely do, my sexy little devil."

I pull my chair right next to Mel's and put an arm around her. Placing my hand under her chin, I turn her head toward me and claim her mouth. Sliding my tongue into her mouth, I leave no doubt of what I want. My dick stirs when I hear her soft moans while we kiss. After I extinguish the campfire, we head inside.

"Now, I wanna see you strip for me," I say.

"Nope."

"Nope? And why not?"

"I'm in charge tonight, so you'll do as I command," she says.

Holy fuck. "As you wish, my love."

"That's a good cowboy. Now, get that hot ass into the bedroom," she commands.

Damn, this is gonna be fun!

CHAPTER 14

Mel

"Rise and shine, sleepyhead," I whisper to the naked cowboy stretched out next to me. He stirs and I shiver when I feel those sexy muscles ripple against my skin.

"Good morning, beautiful," he says, his voice raspy from a good night's sleep. "Last night was incredible. I need to let you be in charge more often."

"Mmm, I quite enjoyed it myself."

"Yeah, anyone within a hundred-mile radius knew that."

"I can't help my cowboy's packin' one hell of a hot dick."

His deep laugh fills my ears as I feel a light swat on my ass. "Naughty, naughty, my devil."

"And what would you like your devil to prepare for breakfast?"

"Stay here and relax. I got that covered."

"A woman could get used to this."

"Well, you better. I intend to take care of you for the rest of our lives."

Judd gets out of bed, and not bothering to pull any clothes on, heads out to the kitchen. My eyes stay locked on his naked ass until he's out of sight. I can't help but smile when I think about what he said. That would've scared me before, but now it's exactly what I want. As I lay there, I think about all the dirty stuff we did last night, and formulate a plan for his birthday. Talk about a night he's never going to forget!

"Breakfast is served, my love."

I look over and see Judd standing there in just an apron, holding a tray of food. After putting it on the night table, he walks over and props my pillows against the headboard I held onto for dear life last night. I sit up and watch as he sheds the apron and gets back in bed. He lays the tray between us and we enjoy a delicious breakfast of scrambled eggs, bacon, and toast. After we cleanup the food and ourselves, we get ready to head out for our adventure.

The walk to the lake is stunning. The walking path has trees and beautiful fields of wildflowers on either side of it. I stop to snap a couple of photos of the flowers. Their multitude of colors takes your breath away. As amazing as the walking path was, when I see the lake, I gaze at it, unable to speak. The sun dances as the crystal clear water lightly ripples from the warm breeze. Bright green blades of grass join in the dance. I snap a couple more photos, never wanting to forget how stunning of a view I'm witnessing.

Benches and picnic tables surround the lake and there's also a dock for launching small row boats. We walk to one of the empty picnic tables and put our stuff down.

"What do you think?" Judd asks.

"Stunning. Thank you for bringing me here. I especially love that house on the other side of the lake."

"I've come here quite a few times by myself when I needed to get away. But now, I'm grateful I get to share this with you."

"Mmm, me too."

We spend a couple of hours fishing, stopping around noon to enjoy the delicious chicken salad sandwiches Judd made. This man truly does spoil me. The sun continues to glow, and the weather is unusually warm for early April. I look at my phone and see that it's eighty-five. Grabbing a paper towel, I wipe the sweat from my forehead.

"How about a swim to cool off?" Judd asks.

"Are you allowed to swim in the lake?"

"Yeah."

I watch Judd's jaw drop as I remove my t-shirt and denim shorts, revealing a bright yellow bikini.

"Damn, baby, you're hotter than the sun!"

Judd strips down to his swim trunks and I almost fall over. It doesn't matter how many times I've seen this man naked, he still takes my breath away. Judd grabs me, carries me down to the lake and deposits me in the water, before jumping in himself. I splash his face and race away from him, but I'm no match for his powerful arms and legs, and he quickly catches me.

"No fair. You're stronger than me."

"And yet, one look from you can bring me to my knees."

Judd picks me up so we're face to face. I wrap my arms around his neck, while my legs lock around his waist. Leaning in for a kiss, I jam my tongue into his mouth and feel his dick stir.

"My, my, someone just woke up," I tease.

"Thanks to my sexy little she-devil."

"I wish the lake was private."

"Oh, and why might that be?"

"As if my horny cowboy doesn't know exactly what I'm thinking."

"I think you need another dunk in the water to cool off, baby."

Before I can respond, I'm in the water again. This time, I'm playing dirty. I take a deep breath and go underwater. I swim to where Judd's standing and yank his trunks down, then take off, resurfacing on the other side of the lake. I see him reach under the water and pull his trunks off. In a few quick strokes, he reaches me and gives me a stern glare.

"You might be stronger, but I'm sneakier," I tease.

Judd's glare changes into a smile and then laughter as he splashes me and takes off. I chase him and finally catch him when he stops near the dock. Sliding my hands up and down his chest, I say, "I think we need to go back to the cabin. Now!"

"Mmm, I think you're right. I need to get you outta that bikini."

We swim over to where our stuff is and get out. Judd wraps me in a towel. After we both dry off and get dressed, we walk back to the cabin. The sun's past its high point, so the walk back is cooler. We sure didn't stay cool long once we got to the cabin. After a much-needed nap, Judd grilled us some chicken for dinner, which we enjoyed around the camp-fire with some homemade potato salad and a bottle of Moscato.

"So, I know we have to head home tomorrow, but will we have time to do something first?" I ask.

"Depends on what."

"I'd love to go see that lake house up close, if we're allowed."

"Yeah, I think we can."

"Yay. It's so gorgeous. I wanna get some pictures. I love old stone covered houses like that."

Judd nods, but says nothing. What's he up to now? We spend the rest of the evening sharing stories from our childhoods. I can't help but notice that all of Judd's center on the years his mom was still here. My heart breaks again when I think how young he was when he lost her, and especially how. In some ways, I understand. If only I could bring myself to tell him about my father.

The next morning, we hike up to the lake house for a closer look and it's even more stunning up close. The porch wraps all the way around the house. The back of the house features an expansive back yard and a barn, as well as beautiful flower gardens and a gazebo. We finish our tour of the property and start the walk back to our cabin.

"It doesn't look like anyone lives there," I say.

"I was thinking the same. Maybe it's just a vacation rental."

"Makes sense."

Judd takes my hand and says, "It's definitely beautiful. Like you."

"Why, thank you, my sweet and handsome cowboy."

When we reach the lake, Judd says, "Let's stop for a bit."

He leads me to one of the benches. As we're sitting and gazing out at the water, Judd puts an arm around me and pulls me in tight.

"My sweet Melissa, thank you for sharing this weekend with me."

"It was my pleasure, my sexy Judd."

"So, you really like the house?"

"Actually, I love it."

I hear Judd's cell ping. He looks down, a smile on his face. Now what's he up to?

"Come with me," he says as he takes my hand. He heads back to the lake house.

"Why are we going back?" I ask.

Judd smiles but doesn't answer. There's a car in the driveway. When the driver sees us, he gets out and approaches us. "Mr. Walker?" he says.

"Yes, pleasure to meet you, James. This is my girlfriend, Mel."

"It's a pleasure," James says, extending his hand.

Accepting his handshake, I say, "Nice to meet you, too."

"Let's finish this," James says to Judd and they walk over to his car. James opens his briefcase and hands a packet of paper and pen to Judd. James points at a few places throughout the packet. I watch Judd sign where James directs him. When Judd's done, James returns the papers to his briefcase and hands a set of keys to Judd. They shake hands again before James gets in his car and drives away.

Judd walks back to me and grabs my hand. He places the keys in my hand. "Happy belated birthday, my love."

I just stand there, keys sitting in my hand, unable to form words. "Huh?" is all I can manage.

"This is your belated birthday present!"

"Keys?" I ask, unwilling to believe what I think my gift is.

"No, silly. Come with me."

We walk together up to the front door of the lake house. Judd takes the keys from me and unlocks the front door. Scooping me up into his arms, he carries me inside.

"So, baby, what do ya think?" Judd asks.

"I-i-is this really for me?"

"Well, really for us, but yes."

"Oh, Judd. I'm speechless. This is amazing. Thank you."

"My pleasure, sweetheart. Now, we'll have a place for vacation any time we want it."

I throw my arms around Judd's neck, crushing my lips to his.

"I've been working on this since the Monday after Lexi's party. James called me at the beginning of the week to let me know my offer was accepted, so we arranged to sign the papers this weekend."

"How did you manage to keep this secret?"

"It wasn't easy, but I was determined to surprise you today."

"You're truly the most incredible man ever. I can say with one hundred percent certainty this is the best gift I've ever gotten."

"Plan on spending a lot of weekends up here."

"I can't wait. When are we coming back?"

"Soon, I promise. But, for today, we need to head back."

"Can't we stay? Please!"

"You have to work tomorrow, honey."

"Eh, the hell with my job," I joke.

"You're so damn cute, my love."

As we're riding back to reality, part of me wants to scream out for Judd to take us back to the lake house.

Judd's voice interrupts my daydream. "What'cha thinkin' about, sweetie?"

"Just wishing I was like Lexi."

"How so?"

"No job to worry about. You could have spent more time away if not for me."

"That's not true. Yeah, I have someone to take care of the horses when I'm away, but that ranch is my job. And I love the life we're building together."

"Just when I think I couldn't love you more."

"You're stuck with me now, you sexy little devil."

"Good thing. This devil sure does like riding her cowboy."

After we get home and unload the truck, we're sitting out by the garden when Lexi comes over, shoulders hunched. "I'm sorry," Lexi says. "I shouldn't have treated you like that at dinner the other night."

"I'm sorry, too. I shouldn't have kept anything from you."

"Let me make it up to you. How about dinner tonight?"

"I'd love to."

"Okay. How about Palermo's at five?" Lexi asks.

"Sounds great."

After Lexi and Damien head home, Judd grabs me and says, "Have I told ya how sweet you are?"

"Yeah. And when I get home, you'll find out how spicy!"

That earns me a playful smack on the bottom as we go inside. "Mmm, I hope I get more of that later, cowboy!"

And when I got home from dinner, I sure as hell did!

CHAPTER 15

Judd

I'm just getting dinner in the oven when I hear Mel's car pull into the garage. My heart still races every time she comes home.

"Mmm, what's that delicious smell?" Mel asks when she comes in.

"Garlic ranch chicken."

"Wow, that smells divine. I'm so spoiled."

"You deserve it, my love."

"Okay, you really need to stop being so sweet!"

"I can't help it, baby. I just love you so damn much. Now, go get in your comfies while I finish dinner."

She flashes her bright smile and my insides melt. Damn, how did I get so lucky? Mel comes back down and all I can do is gawk. Even in a t-shirt and sweatpants, she's the sexiest woman in any room. I look down and see she's barefoot, those sexy little feet with their red toenails. Part of me wants to throw her over my shoulder and take her right to bed.

"Earth to cowboy. Where were you just now?" she teases.

"I bet you can guess, darlin'," I say.

"Well, I'm thinking we wouldn't need clothes."

"We have a winner."

After dinner, we walk down to the garden and sit on the bench.

We're sitting there kissing when I hear Damien yell, "Get a room, will ya?"

I'm enjoying my sexy devil's lips too much to break the kiss, so I ignore Damien. Mel's fingers find my hair, and I feel my dick stir. I talk myself down, and finally come up for air.

"Damn, girl," Lexi says. "We saw the smoke and thought we better check it out."

"Funny," Mel says.

"Care to join us?" Judd asks.

"In that?" Damien exclaims and we all laugh.

"No asshole, I just meant to hang out."

"Thanks, but we're getting ready to head down to the club. We like to pop in unannounced every so often to make sure the staff is performing to our standards," Lexi says.

"Makes sense," Mel says.

"Besides," Damien adds, "I believe you two have other business to handle."

Another round of laughter ensues before Damien and Lexi head out.

We spend a couple hours doing just that.

* * *

"Happy birthday, sexy cowboy." Mel's voice wakes me.

"Thank you, my love," I say, stretching.

"What does the birthday boy want for breakfast?"

"How 'bout you, baby?"

"No, no. I'm your dessert for later," she teases.

"Why can't I have my dessert and eat her too?" I joke.

"Naughty, naughty cowboy! I have plans for you later," she says, licking her lips and rubbing her hands together.

I have a feeling I'm in for one hell of a night! "Well, then, I would love some French toast."

"My pleasure," she says. After a kiss that wakes my dick up, she bounces out to the kitchen. The scent of coffee and vanilla carries me to the kitchen, but of course, all I can think about is getting a taste of that beautiful woman. I want nothing more than to put her on that counter and taste her sweet pussy, but she did promise I'd get her for dessert later. After breakfast, we shower together.

Mel gets home, arms full of bags, none of which she'll let me peek in.

"If I catch you peeking, no dessert later," she warns with a wink.

"That's a fate worse than death."

"Damn right it is!" She gives me a swat on the ass, and of course, my dick twitches. Down boy. She'll play with you later. I watch my sexy goddess get to work on dinner in the kitchen. She banishes me from helping since it's my birthday, so I sit and enjoy the view instead. The kitchen smells amazing, filled with the scents of filet mignon, roasted potatoes and spinach. After we enjoy our decadent dinner, she does a quick cleanup in the kitchen.

"Okay, birthday boy, get your ass on that couch. Now!"

Fuck, I love when she takes charge. I watch as she reaches into her jeans pocket and pulls out a black cloth. She walks behind me and covers my eyes, tying it behind my head. I can't see a thing and the anticipation of what's coming next has me hard as a rock.

"I'll be back soon with your special birthday surprise. And for the record, I'm in charge tonight."

I sit quietly, my heart threatening to beat out of my chest. My dick is threatening to rip a hole right through my pants. I hear her return a little while later. I know by the sound of her steps that she's now wearing high heels and, if possible, my dick gets even harder.

"Okay, my naughty birthday cowboy, you can remove the blind-fold," she says in the sultriest voice I've ever heard.

"HOLY. FUCKING. HELL." Literally.

I can't even remember my name right now as I stare at her, jaw on the floor. Before me stands my naughty little devil. She's dressed in a red lace bra and panties. Garters attached to her panties hold up her red thigh-high stockings. She rests her left hand on her hip while her right hand twirls her devil's tail. Her long blonde hair is curled and cascading down her shoulders. Finishing her look, she's sporting red lipstick, devil horns, and red high heels. I hope that lipstick ends up on my cock later.

She saunters over to the stereo and all I can think about is taking a bite out of that sexy little bottom as I watch the tail sweeping across her ass. I hear *I Touch Myself* by The Divinyls. Mel dances for me and damn, I can barely sit still.

"Behave yourself, cowboy, or you'll be touching yourself."

"You really are a naughty little devil."

"Just you wait. Now, get that hot ass in the bedroom. Move it! Don't keep me waiting," she commands.

Turning on the after-burners, I run into the bedroom. She saunters in behind me, extra sway in her sexy hips. Looking me up and down, she sits in the chair across from the bed and spreads her legs. It's then that I realize her panties are crotchless.

"Strip for me, cowboy. Slowly. And I damn well better enjoy it."

She licks her lips as I slowly remove my clothes. I almost blow my load when I see her teasing her own clit as she watches me. Watching her get off from watching me is so fucking sexy. When I'm completely naked, she says, "She-Devil is quite pleased. Now, get that hot naked ass on the bed. Good. Now, up against the headboard."

She sashays over to the bed, silk scarves in her hand. "That's my good cowboy." She grabs each wrist and ties me to the headboard. My dick's at full attention and aching for her. Hands, mouth, pussy, I don't care right now as long as some part of her touches me. My sexy red-hot little devil.

She kneels on the bed in front of me and opens my legs. She crawls until her face is hovering over my dick. Fuck, I want those pretty red lips wrapped around me. As if she can read my mind. She smiles, then takes my entire length down her throat. She moans as she sucks me hard and fast, quickly sending me over the edge. She lifts her head, locks eyes with me, and swallows every last drop of me.

I watch as she slides up my body, the feeling of lace against my skin driving me wild. Lying on top of me, she nibbles on my ear lobe before moving to my neck. She sucks me hard, and fuck, it feels so good. Her mouth claims mine, kissing me harder than ever before. She twists her tongue around mine, moaning into my mouth.

"She-Devil wants her pussy eaten. Devour me, my cowboy."

"Yes, ma'am."

She kicks her shoes off and stands over me, legs spread, bracing herself on the headboard. I cover her sweet little pussy with my mouth, licking and sucking hard as she writhes her hips. Fuck, this view is amazing, and she tastes so damn good. I have her screaming in no time as she explodes in waves of pleasure, legs shaking as she holds on for dear life.

She lays back down on top and slides back down my body. Straddling me, she sits upright, grabs my dick, and lowers her pussy, still slick from her orgasm, claiming my entire cock. Sitting perfectly still on my dick, she takes her bra off and flings it aside. Fuck, I love those sexy breasts. Leaning forward, she frees my wrists.

"You will spank me while I fuck you," she commands.

"Your wish is my command."

"Damn right it is, cowboy."

Fuck, I love this side of her. She presses her chest against mine as she slides her pussy up and down my shaft. "Spank me now!"

I lightly paddle her hot little ass as she fucks my cock, and fuck this feels incredible. I love the way her lace panties feel rubbing against me. She sits up straight, and I can't take my eyes off her tits as she bounces like a wild woman. She screams as she soaks my cock and that sends me over the edge.

"Now you're going to watch me pleasure myself," she commands. I watch as she grabs her most powerful vibrator, a smaller vibrator, and edible lube out of our dirty drawer. She sits down in the chair and swings one leg over each side, giving me a perfect view of that sweet pussy. She lubes up the larger vibrator, turns it on, and slides it inside her pussy. She takes the smaller one and presses it against her clit. My dick's hard again and I reach for it.

"No, no, no, cowboy. You don't get to touch that cock until I tell you to!"

Fuck!

I watch her slide the vibrator in and out, her eyes locked on mine as she moans. Fuck, this is the sexiest thing I've ever seen. She throws her head back and screams. And that's when I see the most incredible thing ever. She comes hard, her pussy squirting clear across the room.

"Damn, She-Devil, that was so fuckin' hot."

"Good. Now, get over here, and fuck me."

"Ya sure you can take more?"

"How dare you question the She-Devil's pussy? Turn around and bend over."

I feel her hand swat my ass. "You gonna question me again?"

"No ma'am!"

"Good answer. Now face me and get that dick inside me." She reaches down, grabs my cock and lines it up with her sweet hole. I slide into her slick pussy with ease. "Harder, cowboy."

I pound her hard and fast and fuck, she feels so damn good.

"That's it, my sexy cowboy. Pound that pussy. I see you looking at my tits. You want your cock between 'em, don't ya."

"Oh god yes, woman."

"You will address me as She-Devil. Turn and bend over."

Happily, I turn around and get another swat on my ass. Fuck, I love her like this. "Mmm, spank me again, She-Devil."

"Mmm," she moans as her hand again connects with my ass. "Now, get that cock between my tits. I slide between her sexy breasts as she pushes them together, and I feel like I've died and gone to heaven.

"Fuck, I'm about to come," I growl.

"In my mouth. I wanna drink you again."

She opens wide, leans forward, and sucks my dick until I come right down her throat. "Fuck, this night's been incredible," I say.

"Mmmm, but it's far from over. If cowboy can handle more."

"God yes."

"Good. Then I want you to make me come again."

"How, my She-Devil."

"That sexy tongue."

"Mmmm." I kneel before and bury my head between her sexy thighs. She takes her fingers and spreads herself wide, inviting my tongue into her wetness. I run my tongue up her pussy, and I taste a combination of strawberry lube and her tangy juices. She's intoxicating, and I can't get enough. I lightly suck on her clit and she bucks her hips.

"Harder, cowboy, oh fuck." Her body quakes as I send her into orbit. Her chest heaves as she explodes, holding onto the chair until her knuckles are white. "Damn, you know how to please She-Devil," she moans breathlessly. "But now, I want you to carry me to bed, climb on top of me, and make love to me. Slowly. I want it to last, baby. I can't get enough of my big, strong, sweet, sexy, naughty cowboy."

"Can I make a request?" I ask.

"Mmm, yeah."

"I want you completely naked. I only wanna feel your soft skin."

"Oh, Judd. One condition. You have to strip me."

"With pleasure."

I carry her over to the bed and lay her down. "Lift that sexy little bottom." I slide her panties off. One at a time, I remove her stockings, caressing her gorgeous legs as I go. I gaze at her, makeup smeared all over her face, sweat-soaked hair plastered to her head. Yet, she's still a goddess, lying there in all her naked glory.

Slowly, I enter her. We spend the next glorious hour with arms wrapped around each other, bodies pressed tight until we come together. Waves of pleasure consume us, our bodies one in every way.

"I love you, Judd," she whispers.

Moving next to her, still holding her tight, I say, "I love you too. This is by far the best birthday I've ever had. Thank you, She-Devil."

"My pleasure, cowboy. But we're not quite done. Wait here."

"Not sure I could move if I wanted to."

She giggles and walks out of the bedroom. When she returns, she's carrying a small cake with a few lit candles. Her angelic voice sings happy birthday, and my heart skips a beat or ten.

"Make a wish."

"It already came true."

"Eek, thanks for remembering my favorite movie ending."

I blow out the candles and she cuts two big pieces of cake, necessary fuel after the workout we just had. The cake does nothing to replenish our energy, so we use what little we have left to crawl into bed and quickly drift off to sleep.

CHAPTER 16

Mel

I'm just getting ready to head home when my cell rings. I look down and see Tammy's name.

"Hey, girl," I say.

"Hey. Got any plans on Saturday?"

"No. Something happening at the Moon?"

"Yeah, a wedding, so Nick gave us all a night off with pay."

"A wedding?"

"Yeah, friends of his don't have a lot of money and can't afford a venue for their daughter's wedding, so Nick's letting them use the saloon free."

"Aww, that's so great of him."

"Yeah, he's a good guy. Thought maybe a group outing might be fun."

"And I bet you want me to ask a certain somebody."

"How did ya know?"

"Girl, I could see the way you were checkin' him out. I'll be glad to invite him."

"Thanks. Allie and Dane too?"

"I'll ask Allie if they're free."

"Awesome. I hope this isn't a problem, but I'd love to check out BYOB."

"I'm cool with that. I can't let what happened with Lexi rule my life."

"Great. How about we all meet there at six?"

"Sounds perfect. Can't wait."

After I disconnect with Tammy, I call Allie and Jay into my office. They're both on board, so we all agree to meet at six, like Tammy suggested. As we're all walking out to the parking lot, my phone rings again.

"Well, I can tell by your face who that is," Jason teases.

"Hey, sexy cowboy," I say.

"Hey, gorgeous. Called to see if you wanted pizza for dinner."

"Sounds good for a change."

"Great. Figured we'd take a break from cooking.

"Cool. I'll grab it on my way home."

"I have beer and wine coolers chilling."

"You spoil me."

"Because I love you."

"Love you too."

Allie and Jay hit me with a simultaneous, "Awww." I flip them off and we all laugh as we part ways. I grab my phone when I'm in my car and call Palermo's. Judd's waiting on the porch when I get home. He grabs the pizza and greets me with a sexy kiss.

"What made you decide on takeout?" I ask.

"Work's had you stressed recently, so I thought a relaxing evening of pizza, adult beverages and your favorite eighties movies was just what you needed."

"Have I told you lately how amazing you are?"

"It's my superpower."

"Among other things."

"That's my dirty She-Devil."

I can't help but smile, thinking back to Judd's birthday. I never knew I had that level of naughty in me, but that damn cowboy awakened that part of me. And holy shit, it's been incredible. Judd grabs the pizza and carries it to the coffee table. I follow with paper plates, a beer for him, and a wine cooler for me.

"I thought we'd start with a rom-com, then some action," he says.

"Sounds perfect," I say.

We scarf down some pizza and cuddle on the couch to watch Sixteen Candles and Top Gun.

"I have another surprise for you. Come with me," Judd says. He walks me out back and I see a new enclosure on the patio. Judd opens the door and I see a brand new hot tub. And there's a giant rubber duck floating in it!

"When did you do this?"

"I had it delivered today."

"I love it, especially that it's totally private. And, oh my god, thank you for the duckie!"

"I'm glad. Go ahead and get naked, love. I'll be right back."

I strip down and climb into the tub. The warm water feels good against my skin. Judd returns with a bottle of wine and two glasses, along with a plate of strawberries. He strips down and damn, I never tire of seeing that man naked. He joins me and turns on the jets. I sigh as I feel any last bit of stress I had melted away.

"Have a strawberry, my love," Judd says.

"Yum, one of my favorite fruits."

We spend the next couple of hours relaxing in the tub. We polish off the bottle of wine and the strawberries. I plan on spending as much time as possible out here.

"Oh, by the way, I saw that BYOB is having eighties karaoke on Saturday," Judd says.

"Wow, even better."

"Got somethin' in mind?"

"Yeah, if Tammy and Allie are game, I've always wanted to do *Venus* by Bananarama."

"If you're up for two, I'd love to duet."

"Of course. Maybe you, Jay, and Dane could also do a group one."

"Yeah. Can I ask somethin' though?"

"Of course."

"Are ya sure you'll be okay going there?"

"Yeah. I'm not gonna let her keep me away."

"That's my girl. Just don't wanna see you hurt."

"I know, and thanks."

"Sweetheart, you look tired. Ready to turn in?"

"Yeah. I'm exhausted."

Judd gets out and wraps a towel around his waist. He helps me out and wraps me in a towel, then his arms.

"You always seem to know exactly what I need, cowboy."

"Because you're not only my soulmate, you're my heart-mate."

"I've never heard heart-mate before."

"Me either, but I was thinkin' about you earlier, and it popped into my head."

"Well, I love it. And I definitely agree. I'm completely in love with you."

Judd doesn't answer, just covers the hot tub, and I panic. Did I push too hard? Shit. Without a word, he scoops me up in his arms. "I'm in love with you, too, my angel."

Panic is over. Judd carries me to our bedroom, lays me down, and opens my towel. When he pulls his towel off, I smile when I see who's ready to play.

"I think he needs a name," I say, pointing at his dick.

"Is that so? Well, go ahead, name him."

"Thor."

He lays next to me and says, "Well, then, how about he takes you for a ride?"

"Mmmm, yes, please."

Jason stopped by my office the next day to see if I wanted to grab lunch. He doubled over when he saw me walk.

"And just what, or should I say who, were you riding last night?"

"Shut it, dickhead. Besides, it was more than worth it!"

"Seriously, girl, you deserve this happiness."

"Thanks, my friend. Now it's your turn."

"Nah. I'm a lone wolf."

"That's only because you haven't met your she-wolf."

"Hey guys, mind if I join you," Allie says as we're waiting for the elevator.

"Of course not. I wanted to run something by you, anyway."

"Somethin' you need me to do?"

"Oh, not something work-related. How about you join Tammy and me for a song on Saturday? I was thinking Venus."

"Bananarama?"

"Yeah."

"That sounds fun. Count me in!"

"Awesome. And Jay, Judd thought maybe you, Dane, and him could do something too."

"I'm in," Jay says.

"I'm sure Dane will too," Allie says.

"Yay, this is gonna be a blast," I say.

* * *

Friday morning, I'm in my office working on budget reports when my favorite little dickhead appears in my doorway.

"May I help you?" I ask.

"No, just making sure you're working."

I'm about to respond when my intercom buzzes. "Yes, Allie."

"Mr. Donnelly is here to update your computer," Allie says.

"Please, send him in," I say.

"Just remember, you can be replaced," Daniel says and storms out.

Allie races in as soon as he's gone. "I hope it's okay that I called Jason."

"I can't thank you enough," I say. "And I've never been happier to see you."

Daniel reappears in the doorway, so I say, "Okay, so I'm all set with the update?"

"Yes, just call me if anything happens and I'll check it."

"Thank you, Jason."

He nods and walks out of my office, stopping long enough to shoot daggers behind Daniel's back.

"Something you need?" I ask.

"Yeah, this office occupied by someone else."

"Did I do something to you?"

"Duped my uncle into thinking you're worth something."

"Oh, and exactly how did I do that? Your uncle has never complained about my work. If I was so horrible, why was I promoted several times during my career, making it all the way to being an executive."

"Whatever. Just remember, I'm watching you. If you slip up even slightly, your worthless ass is gone."

I never have time to respond before he stomps out like a petulant child.

I stop by Allie's desk on my way out. "Thanks for the save today," I say to her. "See ya tomorrow night."

She smiles and waves, fanning herself behind Judd's back. Judd and I walk to the parking lot together, separating when I reach my car. He pulls out behind me but I lose him at a red light. After I park in the garage, I sit on the porch and wait for him. The words that Daniel spit at me run through in a loop through my head, leaving me feeling down.

A little while later, my favorite pickup truck pulls into the garage. Judd walks over to where I'm sitting and hands me a bouquet of sunflowers.

"What are these for?"

"Because I love you."

"I love you. Thank you."

"How 'bout we go have dinner then spend some time in the hot tub."

"Mmmm, getting naked with my sexy man sounds perfect. I hope Thor wants to come out and play."

"I have a feelin' he will, darlin'. He loves his secret hideout."

Smiling, I look down at Judd's crotch and I swear, I see Thor stirring. After a delicious dinner of turkey tacos, we cleanup and head out to the hot tub. Judd pulls me tight against him and I feel Thor digging into me.

"Well, well, someone's a bit excited," I tease.

"Thanks to a certain pretty blonde she-devil."

"I've yet to hear you protest."

"No way. Being naked with you is my favorite pastime."

"Good, then let's get out of these clothes and in that tub."

"You go ahead. I have a surprise for you," Judd says. The grin on his face has me very excited.

When I hear the opening lines from *I'm Too Sexy* by Right Said Fred, I laugh. Then my sexy cowboy grinds his hips and my jaw drops. He treats me to a strip tease and by the time Thor is unleashed, he's fully erect. I reward the dance with whistles and catcalls. Judd climbs into the tub next to me.

"Mission accomplished," he says.

"Mission?"

"Yeah, to make you smile."

"You're the best! Though I think you were outshined by Thor!"

I'm so hot for my man, I don't even wait for him to make a move. I climb into his lap, facing him, and grab his dick. After a couple quick strokes with my hand, I take him inside me. Water splashes everywhere as I ride him hard and fast, both of us coming quickly. I climb off and sit next to him, sighing loudly.

"Mmm, just what I needed."

"My pleasure, love." Judd turns on the jets and I lean back, closing my eyes. Today's events slowly leave my body, and a feeling of peace washes over me. I lose track of time until Judd looks at his phone. "It's after eleven. I guess we better head inside and get to bed," he says.

"I'm so relieved it's the weekend and I don't have to go to work tomorrow. I hate feeling like this, but Daniel."

"I know. I wish you didn't have to deal with that."

"That's life. But, at least for the next two days, I can put it out of my mind."

"Tomorrow's gonna be fun. Jay, Dane, and I have been chatting. We think you ladies are gonna like what we came up with."

"Oooh, I'm so excited!"

CHAPTER 17

Judd

"Welcome everyone to eighties karaoke night," Scott says from his DJ booth at BYOB.

Though not at our usual VIP table, we're still near the front.

"First up tonight we have three gorgeous ladies for your entertainment. Please welcome Mel, Tammy, and Allie to the stage," Scott says.

I watch the three most beautiful women in the room walk up to the stage. Mel takes center stage, flanked on each side by Tammy and Allie. Venus starts and the ladies start singing and dancing. The crowd goes wild, and rightly so. Mel is a talented singer by herself, but with these two ladies joining her, they rocked the place. The applause was deafening as the ladies hugged and bounced off of the stage. A few other performers sing before Scott announces Jay, Dane, and me. The girls have no idea what we're singing.

I lock eyes with Mel so I can see her face when the song starts. She'll know right away, as Dangerous Toys is one of her favorite hair metal bands. When the opening notes of *Sport'n a Woody* fill the room, a wide smile fills her face. We're sitting at the beginning of the song to hide our naughty little surprise. We stand to sing and I see three mouths drop open.

All three of us have dildos sticking out of the front of our jeans.

144

That got the whole crowd laughing, though I doubt anyone as hard as our girls. When we finished our song, we walked offstage, removed our props, and joined the girls back at our table. All three of them had tears streaming down their faces.

"Oh my god, you guys," Mel squeals. Tammy and Allie are rendered speechless.

"I need to clean my face," Mel announces as she gets up. Allie and Tammy follow her. When the ladies return they're all smiling. Mel and Tammy sit down, while Allie walks over to the DJ booth. When she comes back, she nods at Mel and Tammy. I look at Jay and Dane, both of whom have the same puzzled look on their face.

"Everyone, please welcome Mel, Tammy, and Allie back for a second song," Scott announces.

The girls walk up on stage, and I see a renewed swagger in Mel's walk. Whatever those girls said to her in the ladies' room worked wonders. When the song starts, I almost fall out of my chair. I can't believe my little she-devil is standing on that stage singing Samantha Fox's *Touch Me (I Wanna Feel Your Body)*. My dick is dancing along with her. When I look over at Dane and Jay, they're sitting with their tongues hanging out. When the song ends, they come back to the table with shit-eating grins on their faces.

"Er, I think we need to go home," Dane says, nearly pulling Allie's arm off.

"Have fun, girl," Mel says with a wink.

"Just you wait till I get you home, woman," I whisper.

"Whatever might you be talking about?" Mel says.

"Oh, no, you don't get to sing a song like that, then play innocent with me."

My spidey senses tingle when I see Lexi headed our way, a smug look on her face.

"Damn, girl," Lexi says to Mel.

As we're about to walk outside, Damien stops us. "Mel, I loved that last performance. A lot of tongues waggin'."

"Watch it," Lexi jokingly warns.

Tammy and Mel head outside. I'm about to follow when Damien grabs my arm.

"Leaving so soon?" Damien asks, a shit-eating grin on his face.

"I'm suddenly ready for bed," I say with a wink. Jay and I head out and meet up with the girls. Tammy grabs her cell out of her handbag.

"Would you mind waiting with me until a rideshare comes for me?" Tammy asks.

"Did you already request one?" Jay asks.

"Not yet."

"Then let me drive you home."

"I couldn't put you out like that."

"You aren't. I offered. I'd feel better knowing you get home safe."

"Thanks, Jay."

"Girl, that was hot. See ya Monday," Jay says to Mel. We shake hands before he walks Tammy to his car.

"Hmmm," Mel says, watching them.

"My thought exactly. You okay, sweets?"

"Yeah. I'm over it. Just not gonna put any more effort in. I hope she figures things out, but I can't keep doing this."

"I got ya."

"You always do. Besides, I had a blast with Tammy and Allie. I guess people drift apart sometimes."

The fear that punches me in the stomach hearing her say that is like nothing I've ever felt. "I hope that never happens to us."

"Not possible. You're it for me, Judd. Now, get me home so I can show you."

* * *

Sunday morning, we're enjoying brunch out by the garden

"What do ya wanna do today?"

"How about fishing in the park? It's too beautiful to be inside."

"Ready when you are, my love."

The dock is empty when we arrive at the park, so we claim it. After a couple of hours of fishing and not catching anything, we decide to pack up and take a walk around the park. After we load our gear into the truck, we start our journey around the walking path. When we get to the wooded area, Mel walks over to one of the trees.

"I hate when people dump trash," she says, picking up the large black trash bag sitting there. I hear her gasp as she races to an empty picnic table, so I rush over.

"What's wrong?"

"There's something whimpering in here," she exclaims.

I watch over her shoulder while she quickly opens the bag. We peer inside and two pairs of brown eyes meet our gazes. Mel slowly opens the bag a little more and her eyes well up. She pulls the two little animals out and whispers, "Who could do such a thing?"

I stand there in shock as Mel holds two underweight black labs against her chest. We race them back to my truck and open our cooler. I grab an empty bowl from our gear bag and pour some water in it. One at a time, Mel lowers each dog to the bowl to get a drink. We have an extra chicken sandwich, so she gives each dog a couple of small bites. Mel looks at me, her eyes wet.

"Yes, they're coming to live with us. But first, we need to get them checked by a vet. I'll call mine on the way."

"Thank you," she whispers, her voice cracking.

Doctor Nelson is waiting for us when we arrive. He escorts us into one of the exam rooms.

"Tell me again how you found these two," Dr. Nelson says.

"We were at the park, taking a walk, and Mel saw a trash bag. She picked it up to throw it out and heard whimpering coming from inside," I say.

"That makes me angry beyond words," Dr. Nelson says. "The good news is, both dogs are healthy, other than needing to gain a little weight. Based on their teeth, they're about a year and a half old. What are you planning to do with them?"

"We'd like to adopt them. Is there something we need to do first? Like report them anywhere?" I ask.

"No, you don't. And given how you found them, I doubt anyone's looking," Dr. Nelson says.

We walk out front and schedule a follow up appointment. "What do I owe you for today?" I ask.

"Nothing. You saved these two little angels, so this one's on the house."

"Thank you, Doctor," Mel says.

When we're in the truck, Mel puts the dogs on a blanket between our seats and they curl up together. We drive over to the pet supply shop Hannah owns. Mel wraps the dogs in the blanket and carries them inside. Hannah rushes over when she sees us.

"Who are these two cuties?" Hannah asks.

"We found them in the park. In a trash bag," Mel says.

"Oh my god, how could someone be so cruel?"

"I have no idea. We just left the vet's office, and he said they were fine, so we're here to spoil them."

"Such a good momma. Come with me. We'll get everything they need."

I stand there waiting while Hannah ushers Mel around the shop. A few minutes into their spree, Mikael comes in.

"Hey, Judd."

"Hey, Mikael."

"What brings you in today?"

"Mel and I found two dogs abandoned at the park. Hannah's helping her pick stuff out for them."

"I'll never understand how people can do that?"

"Me either."

"On a happier topic. How are things goin' with Mel?"

"She's incredible. I could talk for days about how much I love that woman."

"That's great. We both miss seeing you two around."

"Not our doing."

"We know."

An awkward silence fills the air as we wait for the girls to finish up. When they finally return, I think Mel has one of everything in the store sitting in her shopping cart. Hannah finishes ringing everything up and when she tells Mel the total, I pull my wallet out.

"I got this," Mel says.

"No way, this is my gift to the new momma," Judd says.

"This one's a keeper, just like Mikael," Hannah says.

"You don't have to tell me that!" Mel agrees.

Mikael helps Hannah bag everything up and helps us get everything loaded in my truck. Hannah and Mikael stand together in front of the store, waving as Mel and I pull away. When we pull into the garage, Mel puts a harness and leash on each dog and walks them to the front yard to handle their business while I unload the bags.

We get their indoor and outdoor training pens set up, then take them outside. We secure them in the pen, which we've put near the garden area, and take a seat on the bench.

"I wanna start training soon, but first, we need to name these two little girls," Mel says.

"Hmmm, I'm not sure."

"They sure do seem to like the garden. Maybe give them flower names."

"I like that idea."

"How about Lily and Daisy?"

"Sounds perfect."

"Yay, now I can get tags made."

"You mean we didn't spend enough at the pet store?" I tease.

Mel's melodic giggle fills my ears and my heart as she walks over to the pen. "Lily," she says. One dog, the one we put a pink collar on, barks. "Then that makes you Daisy," she says to the dog with the teal collar.

"I think they approve," I say. I love seeing Mel with the dogs. All the hurt Lexi's caused her has melted away. I'm a firm believer in the healing power of animals. Rex sure has helped me more times than I can recall.

"I wanna start by teaching them their name, but I wanna separate them for that, so they only learn their own," Mel says.

"Good idea."

"I'm gonna take Lily inside for a little while to start with her."

"Okay, I'll work with Daisy."

After a brief session, Mel brings Lily back outside. "I don't want to overwhelm them with everything they've been through today. Lily did pretty good."

"So did Daisy."

"We can do a little bit more each day."

"Sounds good. I can work with them during the day while you're at work, then you can do some in the evening."

"Perfect. Now, let's get these two little girls some dinner," Mel says.

After dinner, we take the girls for a short walk around the back yard then watch them play with their new toys in the outdoor pen. I watch Mel, the smile refusing to leave her beautiful face. I didn't know it was possible, but I love her even more now. We bring them inside when the sun starts to disappear. They play together inside their pen before curling up and going to sleep.

After all the excitement today, it doesn't take Mel long to fall asleep. After taking the girls outside for a last bathroom break, I carry my angel to bed, get her undressed and climb into bed next to her. Like so many other nights, I drift off to the sweet sounds of my angel's light snores.

CHAPTER 18

Mel

Lunchtime finally rolls around and I'm holding my phone, waiting for Jay and Allie to meet me. I bounce in my chair when they finally join me.

"What's with you?" Jay asks.

"You won't believe what happened yesterday," I say, showing them my phone.

"Oh, they are so cute," Allie squeals.

"I'm guessing there's a story there," Jay says.

"So, Judd and I were walking around the park when I saw a trash bag. I went to pick it up so I could throw it away. And when I did, I heard whimpering. These two sweethearts were inside."

"Oh, that's awful that someone could do that," Allie says.

"For sure, but they have an amazing mom now," Jay says.

"Awww, you big softie," I tease. "This is Lily on the left, and next to her is Daisy."

"I wanna meet them," Jay says.

"Of course. I'll talk to Judd and maybe we can have everyone over."

"How are they health-wise?" Allie asks.

"We took them to Judd's vet, and he said other than them being a little underweight, they were healthy. He gave us feeding instructions to get them back to a healthy weight. Right now, we're working on teaching them their names."

"They're lucky you were there," Jay says.

"Speaking of lucky," I say, "did you get lucky the other night?"

"Melissa!"

"Come on, Jay. I saw the way you were looking at Tammy."

"I drove her home. That's all."

"Seriously? Nothin' happened?"

"Okay, I asked her on a date, but that was all."

"And?"

"We're going out this coming Saturday night. She took a night off of work."

"That's so great," I say.

"I'm so happy for you," Allie says.

"It's just a date."

"Hey, it was just a date the first time Judd, and I got together."

"Same with me and Dane."

"We'll expect a full report Monday morning," I say.

"Yeah, then we can tell you what you did wrong," Allie teases.

"Hey! I'm a stud," Jay teases.

"More like a dud, if you're friends with the blonde birdbrain here." Oh yay, the dickhead's here.

"Back off," Jay warns.

"It's okay," I say. Daniel flashes us a smug look before he walks away.

"What do you mean it's okay," Jay demands.

"I'm filing a complaint with HR when I get back to my office."

"It's about time."

I drive home with the music blasting, trying to put today behind me, I pull into the driveway and see Judd on the porch with Lily and Daisy, and I feel better. After I park, I walk to the porch, and I'm greeted by a passionate kiss and two wiggly butts.

"You okay, sweetie?" Judd asks.

"Always," I say.

He looks at me for a minute but says nothing else. "Dinner's in the oven. Why don't you go get changed?"

"You love spoiling me, cowboy."

"Damn right, baby. I was thinking after dinner, we could take the girls out back to do some more training."

"Sounds good. I have people who wanna come meet them."

"Oh yeah? Who?"

"Jay and Allie. I was thinking maybe we could have them over sometime. Oh, and guess what?"

"What?"

"Jay has a date with Tammy this coming weekend!"

"That's great. I hope she's his Mel."

"Aww, I love that."

"And I love you."

I wrap my arms around my cowboy and squeeze his sexy ass before I go change. After dinner, we're out back when I see Damien and Lexi bring their dogs out. Dave and Maggie run over to the fence and bark. Lily and Daisy answer, so Judd and I walk them over to say hello. Damien smiles when he sees our new family members.

"And where did these gorgeous girls come from?" Damien asks.

I tell Damien about finding the dogs. An angry look fills his face. "What the fuck is wrong with people?"

"That's what we were wonderin'," Judd says. "But we'll help them put their bad start behind them."

"That's nice," Lexi says.

"Yeah, that's Mel. Sweetest gal I've ever met," Judd says.

"Once we finish their training, I'd love it if the four of them could play together," I say.

"Let us know," Lexi says before she and Damien head home.

I go join Judd. Both dogs come to sit in front of Judd and I.

"Without even bein' told," Judd says. "You're an amazing trainer."

"Aww, thanks. Good girl, Lily. Good girl, Daisy." I give them each a treat.

"I think maybe we should try letting them chase a tennis ball," Judd says.

"Okay. I'll go grab a couple."

"No need," he says, pointing to the bin next to the bench. "I moved the garden tools to the garage."

"Those little girls already have you wrapped around their paw, huh?"

"Well, duh, they're sweethearts, just like their momma."

"Poppa's pretty damn sweet himself."

"I thought I was spicy."

"Oh, you definitely can be, and damn, am I grateful."

"Is that so?"

"Oh yeah, the incredible things you do to me in bed. Holy shit!"

"That's my naughty little she-devil. Wait till I get you in bed later."

"Can't wait!"

Grabbing a couple of tennis balls from the bin, I tell both girls to stay, then throw both balls. Neither dog moves.

"Lily. Release," I command. Lily runs and grabs one of the balls.

"Daisy. Release." Daisy joins her, grabbing the other ball.

"I wanna make sure they listen to both of us. Tell them to come one at a time," I say.

"Daisy. Come." Daisy trots to Judd, a tennis ball still in her mouth.

"Lily. Come." Lily runs back, also carrying a ball.

Judd hands them each a treat.

"Hey, where's my treat?"

"You'll get yours when we go to bed!"

"Mmmm, Judd."

We take the dogs inside and they curl up together, quickly falling sound asleep. We sit on the couch so we can ogle them like the proud parents we are.

"Thanks for letting me bring these girls home."

"No need to thank me. I love all three of my ladies."

"I love you so much. And when we go to bed, I'm gonna show you."

"Damn, woman! Let's go."

Judd stands and before I can get up, I'm being lifted over his shoulder. He races us to the bedroom. We strip in record speed and we spend the next hour screaming every filthy word known to man. We may have even made up some new ones!

"What do ya think about skippin' town this weekend?" Judd asks as we're lying in bed.

"What'd'ya have in mind?"

"Takin' the girls to the lake house."

"That sounds perfect. And since the weekend after is Memorial Day, what do you think about hosting a cookout on that Saturday so we can attend the town's celebration on Monday?"

"I'd love to. Who were you thinking of inviting?"

"I was thinking Jay, Tammy, Allie, and Dane. But what about the rest of the couples?"

"I'd like to ask them all."

"Daniel came at me again today." I tell Judd the story from lunch today.

"I'm really getting sick of his shit," Judd says.

"Me too. But this time, I filed a complaint with HR. It really has me considering other options. Now, of course, I won't make any rash decisions, but some days, it's hard not to just walk out."

"You have my full decision, whatever you decide."

"Or what's decided for me?"

Judd pulls me in tight and kisses my forehead. This man can melt away anything stressing me out in five seconds flat. As I lie here in his arms, the day catches up with me, and I let out a loud yawn.

"Babe, why don't you get ready for bed while I take the girls out?"

"I'll come with you."

"You had a rough one, so let me do this."

Smiling, I head into the bathroom while Judd shakes his naked ass at me before throwing his boxers on. Damn, that cowboy is one fine specimen. I giggle at my naughty thought. After I wash my face and apply my night cream, I brush my teeth and crawl into bed naked. I can't help but laugh at how much has changed since I met Judd. I would've died before I slept naked, but now, I don't know if I could sleep any other way.

Judd comes back to the bedroom with two dog beds in his hands, and all I can do is laugh. My big, brawny softie. He puts the two beds in the corner and we watch as Lily and Daisy curl up together. Judd gets ready for bed and pulls his boxers off. Damn, his dick is so hot, and climbs in bed next to me. Before he even has the light off, our little girls are sound asleep.

* * *

I make it through the rest of the week unscathed. Judd loads the truck while I change. We grab a quick dinner while the dogs eat, then start the drive to the lake house. I can't wait to see how much fun the dogs have.

"I forgot to tell ya what I got for them," Judd says.

"What?"

"Canine life vests. I wanna see how they do in the lake, but until we know if they can swim, I wanna keep them safe."

"I'm so excited to see how they do."

"So, tell me the truth."

"About?"

"Is there at least a small part of ya that would live there year round?"

"Oh, absolutely. And please, don't think it's because I don't love the ranch."

"I know that. The ranch is even more special to me now that you live with me."

"Truth is, I would live anywhere as long as it's with you. You're what's home to me."

"Yeah, I know what you mean."

After peeking into the backseat, I say, "I think the girls like to ride. They're both out cold."

"I keep thinkin' how lucky it was we were there that day."

"Me too. I shudder to think what the outcome could've been. And interestingly, I hadn't mentioned it, but was thinking I wouldn't mind having a dog again."

"How come you didn't say anything?"

"I didn't feel right. You opened your home to me. I didn't wanna seem like I was takin' advantage."

"It's our home."

"I'll never tire of hearing that."

Judd tousles my hair, sending a chill all the way down to my toes. Even the slightest touch from him sends my body into orbit. Judd pulls into the driveway when we arrive, and I swear the house is even more beautiful. We leash up the dogs since they don't yet know the property, and start carrying our stuff inside. Judd lays their beds down, and they make themselves right at home. Once we have everything inside, I grab the new bed linens we bought and start making our bed.

Judd comes in to help and says, "Baby, I think we may need to christen these new sheets."

"Mmm, naughty cowboy, I think you're right. Just might need to wait until tomorrow."

"Yeah, I'm kinda tired myself."

We finish up and head back to the living room. "Looks like we aren't the only ones tired," I say, pointing at two cute sleepyheads.

"I can't get over how sweet they are. It took me about two seconds to fall for them."

"Same here."

After we finish unpacking, we head off to bed, neither of us budging until two cold, wet noses wake us the following morning.

CHAPTER 19

Judd

"Rise and shine, my beautiful angel."

All I hear are soft moans coming from the other side of the bed. I gently rock her until she rolls over. "You're lucky you're so damn sexy."

"Oh, and why is that?"

"Otherwise, I'd be annoyed that you woke me."

"You could never be annoyed with your cowboy."

"So very true."

"I thought after breakfast, we could walk the dogs down to the lake. It's gonna be warm today, so we could swim."

"Sounds like a perfect day to me."

"A perfect day for our perfect family."

"It's nice to hear you say that."

"I really mean it. It's been a long time since I felt like I had family."

"I'm sorry. I complain about mine, but what you had to deal with is so much worse."

"We've each had our own issues. That's why we need to stick together."

"Forever, Judd. You're my family. You and these two little furballs."

After a light breakfast, we pack up what we need for us and the dogs, then start the walk to the lake. Not a single cloud hides the bright blue sky. A warm breeze has the blades of grass lightly dancing as we walk. The sun shines strong, quickly warming up the day. Walking behind my three girls, I watch Mel's long blonde braid sway behind her, almost in perfect rhythm with Lily's and Daisy's tails. Three cute butts wiggling as they walk makes me chuckle. When we get to the lake, we put our stuff down.

I open our picnic basket and pull one of the yellow daisies out of the bouquet I snuck inside. I walk over to Mel and tuck it behind her left ear.

"You look so beautiful, my love," I say. Her cheeks redden as she smiles. I love that I still have that effect on her. "What do you say we see how the dogs do in the water?"

"Yeah, let's go."

I watch Mel strip down to her swimsuit, a hot pink two-piece that has my mouth watering. We get the life jackets on the dogs and walk them to the lake. We don't even need to coax them, they get right into the water.

"I think they'll be fine," Mel says as she joins them.

I strip down to my swim trunks, Mel's eyes on me. Well, a certain part of me, the whole time. I'm greeted with a whistle as I walk into the lake and join my girls. The dogs chase each other around the lake, splashing and playing. I grab Mel and pull her close.

"Baby, I gotta tell ya, this swimsuit is hot. Thor approves."

"Mmmm. I fully intend to play with Thor later."

"I sure hope so. He's craving his favorite hiding spot."

"Oh, Judd," she says as she splashes me and swims away.

"Hey, what was that for?"

"You and Thor need to cool off."

"Impossible when your woman's sportin' a sexy pink bikini."

"Full disclosure. I really wish I was out of it right now."

"And why would you wanna be naked?"

"To give Thor what he wants."

"Fuck, woman!"

"Exactly. I wish we could fuck right here in the lake."

"Damn, you're one naughty woman."

Her lips crash into mine as her tongue invades my mouth, showing me just how damn naughty she is. Thor responds, leaving me desperate to be inside of her. I feel her hand slide inside my trunks and stroke my cock. Damn, she just keeps getting naughtier and naughtier. But, two can play at this game. I move her bikini bottom aside and tease that pretty little pussy.

She pulls my dick out and grinds against me. I remove my fingers, and she replaces them with my dick. She slowly rides my dick under the water. I don't know if it's the risk of getting caught, or the proposal, but she feels even more incredible today.

"Fuck, you feel so good against my clit," she whispers.

"Baby, everything about you feels incredible," I say as I lose all control and empty myself inside of her.

"Oh, fuck, Judd," she moans as I feel her quake. We stay pressed together for a few minutes, coming down off the high of a naughty little fuck.

"That was just a little preview of later," she says and races away. I catch up to her and we swim to where the dogs are playing. We spend the afternoon playing in the lake with Lily and Daisy. I can't keep the smile off of my face watching Mel with them. Lily and Daisy slow down, so we guide them out of the water.

They lay down together in the sun. Mel and I wrap ourselves in towels and sit with them, letting the sun dry us. We lay back on the warm grass and the girls get up and nestle between us.

Mel giggles and says, "I guess they're makin' sure we behave out here."

"Never thought I'd get cock-blocked by dogs," I joke.

"I'll more than make up for it later, Cowboy. I'm craving a long, slow ride."

"I might make you leave that sexy bikini on when you do."

As we lie together, I hear Mel's stomach growl.

"How 'bout we pack up and head back? I'm sure the girls are hungry, too."

"Okay, but before we do, thank you for an absolutely perfect day today."

"And I have a special dinner planned for tonight."

"Can't wait!"

We get dressed, leash up the dogs, and walk back to the cabin. As soon as we're inside, they curl up together and within seconds, they're a snoring pile of black fur.

"Join me for a shower, my angel."

"Mmm, I'd love to, my cowboy."

I head down to the kitchen while Mel gets dressed. I almost pass out when she comes down barefoot in a short yellow sundress. While I prep dinner, Mel gets Lily's and Daisy's food ready. They finish at record speed and go right back to napping.

"Can I help?" Mel asks.

"Yeah, you can relax and watch me."

"Mmm, I can handle that, sexy!"

I grab the filet mignon I brought and rub it with my special seasoning blend. I heat a cast iron pan and put the steaks in. While they're cooking, I fill a baking sheet with seasoned baby potatoes and put them in the oven. Finally, I fill another skillet with fresh spinach, drizzle it with some olive oil, and let it wilt.

When everything's ready, I make two plates and carry them to the dining room table. I grab two flutes and a bottle of champagne, and pour us each a glass.

"To the woman who gave me her heart. I love you."

"I love you."

After clinking glasses, we each take a sip. I watch as Mel digs into her food. "Mmm, Judd, this meal is delicious."

"Not nearly as delicious as you, my love."

After dinner, I put on some romantic music. "May I have the honor of this dance, ma'am?"

"Why, yes, good sir."

Pulling her as tight against me as I can, our bodies move as one to the rhythm. This woman truly is the other half of me, and I'll never stop being grateful that I found her. All I can think about is continuing this dance in bed. I scoop her up and carry her into our bedroom and set her down. I lift the sundress over her head and, to my delight, she's completely naked underneath.

Dropping to my knees, I worship my beautiful angel. Her long blonde hair cascades over her sun-bronzed skin and she truly is a vision to behold.

"I love when you watch me like this," she whispers.

"Baby, I could gaze at you for the rest of my life, and it still wouldn't be long enough. You're beautiful."

"As are you, my handsome cowboy."

She reaches down and unbuttons my shirt, tossing it aside. Her hands tour my chest and abs. That light, feathery touch awakens Thor with a vengeance. I stand and remove my pants, revealing my lack of underwear. Her eyes darken as a serious look covers her face.

"What do you want tonight, my love?"

"I want you to hold me tight and make love to me. Slow, sensual, passionate love."

"Mmm, my sexy little cowgirl."

I take her hand in mine and walk her to the bed. We climb in and I immediately pull in tight. Crushing my lips to hers, I slide a couple of fingers inside her, but she's already wet for me.

"Please, I need you inside me," she whispers. As much as I love when she commands me in bed, I love this side of her just as much. So tender, so desperate for me.

"Baby, come lay on top of me."

She climbs on and grabs my dick, lining me up with her sweet opening. She takes me inside and lays her chest against mine. Wrapping my arms around her, I hold her tight against me. Her fingers get lost in my hair as we move together. Her lips brush mine as she twirls her tongue around mine. This is the closest to heaven I've ever been to and it's all thanks to my beautiful angel.

We continue like this for hours, just loving each other. Pleasuring each other. Celebrating our engagement in the sweetest, sexiest way two people can celebrate. Her breathing matches mine. Her moans match mine. Her everything matches mine.

"Oh, god, Judd, I'm so close. Please, harder, please, baby."

I thrust harder until I feel her body quaking against mine. She moans as she bucks against me. "Baby, keep riding, please. I need to empty inside you."

She pumps my dick hard and sends me over the edge. "I love you, baby," I cry out as I fill her.

"I love you, cowboy." She doesn't move, completely spent from our passion. She feels so damn good in my arms. I never want this moment to end. She takes my mouth again and I feel her desire as her tongue sweeps through my mouth. Still inside her, my dick hardens again. I roll her onto her side, and spooning her we make love again. My fingers tease her clit while I thrust into her, and she comes quicker this time.

"Mmm, so good, cowboy," she murmurs. After filling her a second time, I'm spent and I slide my dick out, but I keep her in my arms. We lay facing each other, kissing, embracing, just loving being together. My beautiful fiancee.

"I never thought this would happen to me. Never thought someone would love me after what I did. But, baby, you didn't sit in judgment," I whisper.

"Love, you did the right thing. And even if I didn't think so, it was still your decision. I could see the pain in your eyes when you told me. The only thing I could think about was wanting to take that away from you. To hold you and love you until you were whole again."

"And that's exactly what you did."

"Trust me when I say you did the same for me. Thanks to you, I'm starting to see myself as more than just damaged goods that nobody wants."

"Good, because you aren't. That Derek didn't realize what an amazing woman you are is a reflection of him, not you."

"I'll admit, I still slip sometimes, especially when Daniel comes at me, but then I come home, and you remind me."

"And I'll never stop, baby."

The next morning, we treat ourselves to one more romp between the sheets. After a sexy shower together, we have a quick breakfast, pack up and head home. Our fur-kids curl up together on the backseat. Of course, momma has to take a thousand pictures before we go. She's so damn cute.

Mel turns her phone on and checks on the e-vite she sent for our Memorial Day party. "Everyone said yes except Damien and Lexi," she says.

"Did they say no?"

"No response either way. I hope they decide to come."

"Maybe they wanna wait until they can talk to us."

"Could be. I would just hate for them to feel left out."

"I know, same here."

"I can't wait to see all the dogs together!"

"And if I know you, that's the part you're most lookin' forward to."

"Without a doubt."

She lays her head on my shoulder, and I put an arm around her. Mel inches her cute little bottom onto my lap, rests her head on my chest, and within minutes, I hear soft snores. I sneak out from under her and lay her down, covering her with a blanket. Heading into the kitchen, I feed Lily and Daisy, then make dinner for my girl.

We take the dogs out for a bit of play after dinner until the rain starts. We spend the rest of the evening on the couch. Mel lies on my lap while I read to her until she falls asleep. I carry her to our bedroom, get her undressed and tucked in. After I take the dogs out for their last potty, I crawl into bed with my love, falling asleep to the sound of her breathing.

CHAPTER 20

Mel

Monday morning, I'm in my office, hoping against hope I can have a Daniel-free day. After this amazing weekend, I want nothing bringing me down. I want my only challenge today to be trying to hide my ring from Jay and Allie until the barbecue. After running through any new emails that come in, I complete a couple of report requests for the other department heads and get those sent off. I move on to some expense report reviews when Allie buzzes.

"Good morning, Allie."

"Good morning. I'd like to talk with you about something."

"Of course, please come in."

"Do you mind if I shut the door?" Allie asks when she comes in.

"Not at all. What's going on?"

"I wanted to speak with you about a job opening."

"Okay."

"You know I've been working on my degree in Human Resources. Well, I'm finishing my last class this week. I saw a job opening for an HR intern and I'd like to apply."

"Oh, Allie, that's great."

"So, you're not mad?"

"Absolutely not. I'll be sad to see you go, as you've been a dream employee, but I would never hold you back. Do you need me to write a letter or anything? You have my full support."

"I'm not sure. I haven't applied yet as I wanted to speak with you first."

"Then I expect you to go apply as soon as you return to your desk."

"I'll let you know what I need as soon as I know. And thank you so much for being so supportive."

"You've earned it."

After Allie leaves, I get back to work on my expense report reviews, answer a few new emails, and start drafting a letter for Allie in case she needs it. I'm so immersed in my work that I don't notice Jay come to my door until he scares the shit out of me.

"Ready for lunch?" Jay says. I jump and dramatically throw my hand over my heart.

He laughs and says, "What had you so focused?"

"Just checking out the internal candidate pool."

"You're hiring?"

"Possibly. Allie's applying for the HR internship. She let me know this morning."

"Good luck replacing her."

"It's gonna be impossible. I'll be happy if I find someone moderately close to her."

"Yell, if I can help in any way."

"Thanks. Now, I'm starving, so let's head down for lunch." I reach for my handbag.

As we walk to the elevator, Jay asks, "So how was your weekend?"

"Perfect! Judd took me to the lake house this weekend."

"You have no idea how it warms my heart seeing you happy," Jay says.

"What about you? I didn't forget that you had a date this weekend."

"We had the best time. I'm almost hesitant to say it, but I can actually see this going somewhere."

"Wait! The career bachelor is actually considering a relationship."

"Shut it, bitch! Seriously, though, Tammy's special. And hey, you need to know how much your friendship means to her."

"Really?"

"Yeah. She's had some tough times with family and now-former friends tryin' to use her. Sound familiar?"

"Sadly, yeah. I'm sorry she's had to go through that."

"Yeah, both of you. She mentioned a few times how thankful she was to have you."

"Well, anytime she needs an ear, she's welcome to call me."

"I'll tell her when I see her tonight."

"Tonight! Wow, that's great."

"She's really looking forward to your barbecue, too."

"I'm glad. I want you to find that happiness that Judd and I have."

"Never thought I wanted that, but truth is, seeing you and Judd has changed that. I see the way your face lights up at the mere mention of his name. I want a woman to feel that way about me."

"She's out there. You are one of my favorite people ever, and I know you have a lot to offer a woman."

"About nine inches."

"Oh my god. I wasn't talking about your dick, you ass."

"Sorry, couldn't resist. But you're right, she's out there, and I think I found her."

"Jay and Tammy sitting in a tree..."

"What are you, five?" Jay laughs as we reach the front of the line and pay for our food. Allie sees us and waves us over to the table she's sitting at.

"Hey guys," Allie says when we sit down. "Mel, the recruiter already called me and set me up for an interview."

"Wow, that was fast. When is it?"

"Tomorrow afternoon. The recruiter's going to reach out to you, if that's okay."

"Yes, of course."

"If you'd like to practice interviewing, I'm willing to help," I say.

"Do you think you'd both be willing? The recruiter said two people will interview me together, so I'd love to practice that," Allie says.

"Sure, happy to help," Jay says.

"Thanks both of you," Allie says.

"You got it. We'll let you know when we're ready," I say.

Jay and I leave Allie at her desk and head to my office. "Do you have a copy of the newest approved questions?" Jay asks.

"No, haven't had to hire in a while."

"I'll go grab 'em."

"Cool. I'm gonna see if the recruiter assigned to Allie reached out yet." When I open my email, I see she has sent me a few questions. While I wait for Jay, I fill out her questionnaire and write my recommendation. We run through the list of questions, decide who's asking which ones, then call Allie to my office. We take turns asking her every question on the list.

"Will I really have to answer that many questions?" Allie asks when we're done.

"Most likely not. We all usually pick one or two from each category. Not knowing which your interviewer will pick, we decided to ask them all," Jay says.

"Thanks. I appreciate the help."

"You're welcome," I say. "Also, when I got back from lunch, I had an email from your recruiter, so that's taken care of."

Jay looks at his watch and says, "Gotta run. I have a call with a vendor about some new software."

Allie stays after he leaves. "Everything okay?" I ask.

"Yeah. Just feeling a little bad."

"What about, if you want to share?"

"Leaving you."

"Do you want this internship?"

"Very much."

"Then that's all that matters."

"But I've worked for you for so long."

"Yes, and I'm lucky to have had you. But, answer me this. Did you go to school for your HR degree only to keep being my assistant?"

"No. I did it to have a career in HR. It's always been my passion."

"Then there's nothing to feel bad about. I consider you more as a friend, anyway, so nothing is really gonna change between us."

"Thank you, Mel. For everything."

"You're welcome. Now, why don't you head out early, so you're well-rested for tomorrow?"

"Okay. See you tomorrow."

"Have a good evening."

When I get home, Judd and the dogs don't greet me. I see a note on the kitchen table.

Welcome home, my love. Get changed and meet me in the hot tub area.

Love,

Your Sexy Cowboy

I walk to our bedroom and see my pink bikini sitting on the bed. Smiling as I remember his reaction at the lake, I quickly change. The girls are curled up on their bed in the corner. There's a small table set up next to the hot tub. On the table, I see a silver ice bucket with a bottle of Moscato chilling, two glasses, and a fruit and cheese plate.

"A woman could get used to this," I say as I lower myself into the warm water.

"You better. I fully intend to pamper you for the rest of our lives."

"Mmmm," I sigh as I relax from the jets massaging my body.

"How was work today?"

"A little bittersweet."

"What happened?"

"Allie finished her HR degree, and she applied for an internship. I'm so happy for her, but I'm sorry to lose her as an assistant."

"I'm glad for her, but yeah, I understand."

"She was worried I was gonna be upset with her."

"And you, instead, what?"

"Not much."

"Come on, love, I know you."

"I wrote her a glowing recommendation and Jay and I mock-interviewed her."

"That's my angel."

We sit in the tub relaxing until the furries stir and stand near the door leading to the backyard.

"Looks like our cuties need a potty break," I say. I'm about to get up when Judd stops me.

"You relax, I got 'em."

Smiling, I watch as he gets out of the water. His swim trunks cling to his wet body, showing off his glorious muscles. My mouth waters as I watch him head to the back yard with the dogs. Judd returns when the girls are done, and we stay in the tub until dusk blankets the sky. As always, my sweet cowboy gets out first, then helps me out and wraps me in an over-sized towel. We cover the hot tub and head inside.

Instead of chilling on the couch in our jammies, we crawl into bed naked and work on a couple of crossword puzzles together. Call me a dork if you want, but I'd do just about anything if it was naked with my sexy cowboy. Plus, I'm a 'word nerd' and I always loved solving crosswords. We reward ourselves for solving two puzzles with our favorite naked activity followed by a deep, peaceful slumber.

The next few days drag, and I'm thankful Mr. O'Laughlin closes the Friday before any major holidays, so we get an extra-long weekend. Speaking of extra-long, I'm sitting and daydreaming about a certain part of Judd's body when Allie startles me, grinning from ear to ear.

"I hope that smile's for what I think it is."

"I got the internship," she squeals.

I walk over to her and give her a hug. "Congratulations. You deserve this so much."

"They told me the interview was just a formality and that it was your recommendation that sealed the deal. Thank you. Truly, I mean that."

"No need. I only wrote the truth. You earned that."

"I know normally, two weeks is the appropriate notice, but they're hoping I can start sooner. That's your decision, though."

"When do they want you?"

"Right after the holiday."

"What do I need to do?"

"Just reply to the recruiter's email asking what day you'll release me. That would be the last day I work for you."

"Got it. Things are slow today, so why don't you grab some boxes and move into your new desk today? That way, you can start fresh on Tuesday morning."

"Are you sure?"

"I'm about sick of you, anyway," I tease.

"I know I've said this like a hundred times, but thank you."

"I'll see you and Dane on Saturday."

Allie practically floats out of my office while I answer the email and release her on the payroll system. I duck out early on Thursday so I can stop at the grocery store to grab what I need for the picnic. I run to Allie's favorite store, Yankee Candle, and grab a gift for her promotion. Judd's been busy all week getting the backyard ready, so Friday all we have to do is get the food ready and clean the house. We get up early Saturday morning, pleased to see the sun shining in a bright blue sky.

"I'm so excited for tonight," I say while we're finishing a light breakfast of strawberries and vanilla yogurt.

"Me too. Now put your sous chef to work," Judd says. "I love when you order me around, though I prefer it in the bedroom."

"No distracting me today, cowboy."

"But, baby, all I can think about is your naked little ass up on the counter."

I shake my head as I laugh. "If you want to put your fingers in something moist, get the burger patties made."

He laughs and grabs a bowl, then unpacks the beef. I grab the ingredients for the burgers and put everything in the bowl. My body heats as I watch Judd's hands work the meat.

"Do you have any idea how bad I wanna fuck you right now?" I say.

"Holy hell, woman. Just from watching this?"

"Oh yeah. I'm imagining you working my body like that."

"That's it. We're canceling the picnic."

"Ha, ha, cowboy."

After the food's all prepped and packed away in the fridge, we grab showers and get ready for our guests. Lexi and Damien head over once they see us out back. After an on-leash meeting, we let the dogs off leash in the pen and they all become fast friends. As everyone else arrives, we introduce the rest of the dogs. Judd bought a second pen this week, so we had a big enough area for the entire crew, who kept themselves entertained with the far too many toys Judd and I bought. And of course, nobody came empty-handed, so we have enough food to feed our entire small town.

Once the men are done grilling, everyone makes a plate and gathers around the picnic table. Judd and I stand at the head of the table.

"I'm so glad everyone could come today. Allie, can you come up, please?" I say. After she joins me, I continue, "I've be privileged to have this talented woman as my assistant for the last decade. But, now that she's completed her degree in HR, she's moving on to join that team. You're gonna be impossible to replace and I know you'll do great things in your new role." When I finish, I hand her a gift bag.

"You didn't have to do this," Allie says. "Wow, a whole candle assortment. Thank you."

"And now, it's my turn for an announcement," Judd says. "Despite our best efforts to keep this a secret, a few of you found out. But now we can officially tell the rest of you, this beautiful lady agreed to become my missus."

Everyone claps and cheers while I, in typical fashion, tear up. Tammy and Allie practically knock me over with hugs. After a long round of hugs and handshakes, everyone sits down to eat. Once our guests have had their fill, I start carrying the remaining food inside and Tammy joins me.

"I'm so happy for you," she says.

"Thanks. I'm happy for you too."

"Jay's great."

"Yeah, he is. I think I'm fallin' for him. I'm just not sure it's mutual."

I want more than anything to tell her what he said, but it's not my place. "Jay keeps his feelings close to the vest. Just give him time. He's been hurt before, so it takes him a little longer to trust."

"Thanks. I definitely don't wanna push too hard."

After we finish up, we rejoin the party. Now that the food's all put away, he opens the pen so the dogs can wander the yard. The dogs are enjoying playing while us humans are all standing in groups talking. Suddenly, I hear Daisy and Lily give a couple sharp barks and race over to me. They sit down on either side of me and lean against my legs. I've never seen them behave like this and I'm puzzled. That is until Jay points over my shoulder.

CHAPTER 21

Judd

I'm standing near the garden with Damien and Johnny when I see Daisy and Lily race over to Mel. They flank her as if they're protecting her from something. I scan the backyard and suddenly see the cause of their behavior.

"What the hell are they doing here?" I mutter as I walk over to Mel.

I glare at Daniel and Trish.

"Why are you here?" Mel asks.

"I got into a little fender bender," Trish says.

"And?"

"And my insurance lapsed, so I need to pay the damages plus a fine."

"Again, I ask, and?"

"I need money."

"Then get a job."

"I have one."

"Then get another one."

"It would just be a loan."

"You need a loan. Go to a bank."

"They turned me down."

"Not my problem."

"Yes, it is."

"You give me one good reason why it's my problem."

"I'm your sister."

"I said a good reason. You're an adult, you're not my kid, you're not my damn responsibility."

"Not like you can't afford it."

"That's not the point."

I jump in before Trish has a chance to say anything else. "You both need to leave. Now."

Trish crosses her arms and doesn't budge. "We'll leave when we're done," Daniel says.

"Done what?" I say. "Upsetting my girlfriend?"

"Oh boo hoo," Daniel sneers. "You want us to leave? Make us."

Before my brain catches up, my fist connects with his face, knocking the smug little smirk right off of him.

Mel looks down at him and says, "I'd say you're done."

Trish helps him up and they huff off. Before they exit the backyard, Trish turns and says, "This isn't over."

* * *

We're sitting on the couch after the party listening to the dogs snoring away. I put my hand on Mel's shoulder and she looks at me.

"Well, that was eventful," I say.

"That's quite the understatement."

"I know I shouldn't have hit Daniel."

"Eh, he deserved it."

"But what if it costs you your job."

"Then I get another one."

"But what if Trish comes after you."

"Let her. I can handle anything they throw at me as long as I have you."

I hope she's right, but I'd be lying if I said I wasn't worried. There was something sinister in the way Trish told her it wasn't over. Maybe I'm reading too much into it, but my gut has never been wrong before.

* * *

Judd and Mel's story continues in Silent Screams.

Playlist

Is This Love – Whitesnake
Feel Like Makin' Love – Bad Company
If I Close My Eyes Forever – Ozzy Osbourne / Lita Ford
Rubber Ducky, You're the One - Ernie
Animal Magnetism - Scorpions
Total Eclipse of the Heart – Bonnie Tyler
Wait - Steelheart
Soul Soul – Dean Davidson
Mean to Me – Brett Eldredge
Any Man of Mine – Shania Twain
Country Girl – Luke Bryan
Eternal Flame – The Bangles
What Love Can Be – Kingdom Come
I'll Never Let You Go – Steelheart
Stayin' Alive – The Bee Gees
Forever – KISS
I Touch Myself – The Divinyls
Venus – Bananarama
I'm Too Sexy – Right Said Fred
Sport'n a Woody – Dangerous Toys

Touch Me (I Wanna Feel Your Body) – Samantha Fox
Celebration – Kool and the Gang

Acknowledgments

Edited by Heart Full of Reads Editing
Proofread by Alyssa's Book Services
Cover by Carter Cover Designs

About the Author

Samantha Michaels was born in 1973 in the small town of Abington, PA and was raised and still lives in Hatboro, PA (both suburbs of Philadelphia). She is married to her high school sweetheart and they have a rescue dog, a beautiful Black Lab named Holly.

When she's not writing or working at her full-time job, she enjoys watching her Philly sports team (hopefully) win, listening to heavy metal/hard rock music, Texas Hold Em, reading, and spending time with friends and family.

Her love of reading began at a young age, thanks to her mother and Sesame Street. Her mom read to her constantly, and by three years old, she was reading on her own, and hasn't stopped. This eventually turned into a love of writing. She was writing for herself and then for a small group of friends, one of whom told her she should be writing books. She took her friends advice and has since published several romance books with plenty more on the way.

For updates and a free book, click **here** to sign up for my newsletter

Also by Samantha Michaels

www.ingramcontent.com/pod-product-compliance
Lightning Source LLC
Chambersburg PA
CBHW021009180626
46814CB00003B/1213